Readers love

"…an entertaining read. It's quick and sweet, and sure to appeal to fans of country music and rags-to-riches tales."

—Joyfully Reviewed

"If you are a fan of country music this would be a good book to read! If you are a Scotty Cade fan, you'll probably like this one."

—Love Bytes

"*Final Encore* is a great read that will be sure to bring author Scotty Cade many fans."

—Literary Nymphs Reviews

"Mr. Cade certainly knows how to write an enchanting tale with a storyline and characters that are enjoyable to read."

—Long and Short Reviews

By SCOTTY CADE

Acting Out
Forever for Now
The Mystery of Ruby Lode
The Royal Street Heist
Sunrise Over Savannah • Chasing the Horizon
An Unconventional Courtship • An Unconventional Union

FINAL ENCORE
Before the Final Encore
Final Encore
After the Final Encore

LOVE SERIES
Wings of Love
Bounty of Love
Treasure of Love
With Z.B. Marshall: Foundation of Love

Published by DREAMSPINNER PRESS
http://www.dreamspinnerpress.com

After the FINAL ENCORE

Scotty Cade

DREAMSPINNER PRESS

Published by
DREAMSPINNER PRESS

5032 Capital Circle SW, Suite 2, PMB# 279, Tallahassee, FL 32305-7886 USA
http://www.dreamspinnerpress.com/

After the Final Encore
© 2015 Scotty Cade.

Cover Art
© 2015 Reese Dante.
http://www.reesedante.com
Cover content is for illustrative purposes only and any person depicted on the cover is a model.

ISBN: 978-1-63476-252-6
Digital ISBN: 978-1-63476-253-3
Library of Congress Control Number: 2015905042
First Edition July 2015

Printed in the United States of America
∞
This paper meets the requirements of
ANSI/NISO Z39.48-1992 (Permanence of Paper).

To Kell, my husband of nineteen years. Not one of my books would ever see the light of day without your endless support and sacrifice. You pull double duty at our business so I can chase my literary dreams, and I can never thank you enough. I love you with all my heart.

This book also goes out to my late parents, Jean and Julius. They are the inspiration for Jean and Jules James, and I miss them every day. I love you both!

I would also like to thank my editor and friend Andi Byassee. You take my jumbled words and turn them into actual novels, and that is no small feat. You amaze me with every story. XOXO!

And lastly, I would like to thank Reese Dante. She is the spectacular artist who does all my cover designs. I'm always amazed at what she can do with the little guidance I offer her. And... trust me when I say I'm pretty picky when it comes to my covers. I'm proud to call her my friend.

Preface

WELL GANG, we've almost come full circle. *Final Encore* was my very first novel, and as most of you already know, it went through a recent rerelease. Additionally, I released a free read from Dreamspinner Press, called *Before the Final Encore*, to highlight a little of the journey that brought Ian to Nashville. And finally I'm proud to offer the last in the series, *After the Final Encore*. This book deals with the homophobia that is alive and well in Nashville and how Ian and Billy overcome the hurdles to live their lives as proud and open gay men. I hope you enjoy!

Scotty Cade

Chapter One

BRAD PAISLEY and Carrie Underwood stood in the center of the stage, Carrie holding a white envelope with the Country Music Association logo printed on the outside.

"And last but certainly not least," Brad said. "The nominees for CMA's Entertainer of the Year are...." Brad paused and then read the first name, "Miranda Lambert." The camera panned the crowd stopping on Miranda and her husband Blake Shelton, both smiling broadly, Blake holding Miranda's hand.

"Luke Bryan." Brad paused again as they repeated the process.

"Billy Eagan." And suddenly Billy's smiling face was on the JumboTron, with Ian sitting right next to him grinning proudly, and Jean and Jules right behind them, smiling as well.

"Chris Young." Another pause while the picture changed.

"And Jennifer Nettles."

Billy chuckled as Ian's knee rapped his firmly. This sort of innocuous action was something they'd developed early in their relationship to say "I love you" while they were under the ever-watchful eye of the public.

The camera would be on Billy and Ian when they announced his name as a nominee, so he waited until all the nominees were announced before he returned the gesture and added a smile. His heart was pounding as hard as it ever had. It had been a long, hard year. He and Ian had been on tour for the last ten months, and they were both exhausted. They'd been in a different city every couple of days, and they both felt like the Capitol jet was more their home than the Westhaven townhouse they shared in Franklin, Tennessee, north of Nashville.

"And the winner is...," Carrie Underwood said.

Billy's heart stopped as the words left Carrie's mouth.

"Billy Eagan!"

The crowd went wild as Billy and Ian both jumped to their feet. Ian threw his arms around Billy and held on tightly, and Billy returned the embrace. After all, he wouldn't have a career or a life without Ian.

"Congratulations, Cowboy!" Ian whispered as he buried his face in Billy's neck and kissed him quickly. "I love you."

They separated, and Billy hugged Jean and Jules before walking up onstage to accept his award.

Billy made it up the fifteen or so stairs leading to the stage without stumbling, and when he arrived, Brad and Carrie hugged him, and Carrie handed him his third award of the night. He'd already won for Record of the Year and Album of the Year and now Entertainer of the Year. Billy stepped in front of the microphone. He scanned the crowd, but the only people he wanted to see were Ian and Jean and Jules. They were all still on their feet clapping and smiling broadly.

"Oh God," Billy said holding his award over his head and pumping it in the air. "I'm so blessed, I don't know where to start. First of all I'd like to thank all the fans."

The audience roared again.

"You got me here, and I'd be nothing without you." Billy took off his hat and bowed. "Thank you from the bottom of my heart."

He squinted and looked into the first few rows, trying to find Josh. "Next I'd like to thank Capitol Records Nashville for always supporting me." He spotted Josh and Suzie. "And you," he said, pointing at Josh, "Josh Randal. For believing in me and always looking out for me. I love you, man. I want to thank all my family back in New Orleans." Billy brought two fingers to his lips and held them out to Jules and Jean. "And my family here in Nashville, Jean and Jules James. I love you both. Thank you for giving me my big break. And... most of all I want to thank my manager and best friend, Ian Dillon. You found me. You groomed me. And you made me the man and the entertainer I am today. I love you, man."

Ian was still on his feet, smiling so proudly Billy almost lost it.

"Thank you all," Billy said one last time as he turned and exited the stage.

The moment Billy got backstage, a barrage of people surrounded him with congratulations. But the only person he wanted to see was Ian, and again Ian didn't disappoint. Ian never disappointed. He was at Billy's side within minutes, leading him through the crowd to the pressroom, where he had at least another half hour of interviews with all the major networks and some local stations. With the Capitol after-party still to come, they had a long night ahead of them. As they ducked into the private waiting area, Billy took a seat. Before Ian could sit beside him, he heard a soft voice. "Excuse me, Mr. Dillon?"

Ian turned to see a media assistant. "Hi," he said.

"Can I bother you to go over the press list before Mr. Eagan gets started?"

"Sure," Ian said, looking at Billy. "I'll be right back."

"And I'll be right here." Billy watched Ian walk away with the assistant.

While Billy waited, he looked down at the award he was still holding. The events of the night replayed in his head like a slow-motion video camera. The red carpet, his first two awards, Entertainer of the Year, and lastly his acceptance speech. What had stayed with him the longest was the red carpet.

When his limo had pulled up to the Bridgestone Arena, after a quick good luck kiss, he and Ian had quickly gone into public mode out of habit, Ian taking the seat across from him and them touching in no visible way. When the attendant had opened the door, they were immediately on display. People were yelling Billy's name, and flashbulbs were going off from every direction before they exited the limo.

As usual Billy had stepped out of the limo before Ian. But as with all the events they attended together, Billy insisted he and Ian walk the red carpet side by side. After all, without Ian there would be no Billy, and he never forgot that.

Before he got out of the limo, Billy looked down the long red carpet, lined from end to end with representatives of various

3

entertainment networks and radio stations, and he saw other artists strolling along with their husbands and wives, girlfriends and boyfriends, holding hands and showing public affection, stopping and posing arm in arm along the way to have their pictures taken. He wanted so badly to do the same with Ian, but this was Nashville and country music, where being gay was not accepted.

So, as usual, he sucked it up and followed in the footsteps of the other artists. He signed autographs and took selfies with fans until he reached the interviewers. Ian had always chosen to stay in the background until Billy forced him to step up and share the interviews with him. Occasionally they'd pose together for pictures, arms draped loosely over each other's shoulders, but a friend taking a picture with a friend was the extent of their public displays of affection. He was starting to resent the fact they couldn't be themselves, and it was getting harder and harder to pretend to be someone he was not. *I think it's time I talk to Ian about this.*

When Ian returned, he sat down next to Billy and smiled.

"Congratulations, Cowboy," he whispered in Billy's ear again, looking around to make sure no one was in earshot.

"I can't believe this," Billy said, his hands still trembling from the adrenaline rushing through his veins.

"You earned this, Billy. No one in this business worked as hard as you did. Ten months on the road nonstop, and you never once missed a show. Seven number-one singles off your last album alone. Album of the year, I might add. Believe it! You earned it," he repeated. "I'm so fucking proud of you and—" He leaned in close, again looking around for wandering eyes and ears. "—I want to kiss you so badly right now it's killing me."

"I know," Billy agreed. "Me too. I'm sorry, Ian."

"What are you sorry about? It's not your fault Nashville is so damned homophobic."

It's now or never!

"I know it's not my fault, but I—we could try and change it. I mean… all I could think about when we walked the red carpet was how much I wished I could hold your hand to let people know how I feel about you."

"I know," Ian said. "But not at the risk of your career."

"My career won't last forever, Ian. And besides, we have more money than we could ever spend. Why not come out and see if we can try and do our part to change the way Nashville views us? I'm not the only one, you know. There's Ty Herndon and Billy Gilman who both came out recently. And what about Steve Grand? And don't forget Chely Wright. Maybe we can form some type of coalition and all work together to change Nashville."

"We're ready for you, Mr. Eagan," a press assistant said, sticking her head inside their cubicle and interrupting their conversation.

"Please, call me Billy," Billy said, standing up.

"We'll talk about this later," Ian assured him. "Now go get 'em. We have a celebration to get to."

WHILE BILLY did his press interviews, Ian watched him move from network to network, radio station to radio station, talking about his album, the tours, his number-one singles, and his big wins of the night. Everyone shook his hand and patted him on the back like they were his best friends, but no one knew him. Really knew him. Who he was as a person, who Ian was to him, and more importantly, who he was to Ian.

Ian thought about their conversation. He would love to tell the world what Billy meant to him. What they meant to each other. But he couldn't allow Billy to come out. Not now. Not unless he was ready to give up his career. Their relationship would destroy him professionally, a sad but true fact. Nashville was not ready to support homosexual artists. It was amazing how the entire country and world was evolving and standing up for gay rights while Nashville was stuck in the dark ages. *Do the record execs not think they have gay country music fans? If Billy ever gets tired and ready to give up his career, then yes, maybe I'll encourage him to come out. But then and only then.*

"We're done here, boss," Billy said, touching Ian's arm and giving it a quick squeeze. "What's say we find Josh and Suzie and Jules and Jean and head over to the Capitol after-party?"

"Your carriage awaits, Cinderfella," Ian said, bending at the waist and moving his hand in a sweeping motion. "After you."

"You're such a dork sometimes," Billy said teasingly.

"But I'm your dork," Ian whispered.

Billy winked. "And don't you ever forget it."

"Not a chance, Cowboy."

ON THE short ride from Nashville's Bridgestone Arena to Sambuca, where the Capitol Records after-party was being held, Billy's limousine was filled with an indescribable energy. He and Ian were sitting next to each other with Ian's arm thrown casually over the back of Billy's seat in a protective but nonintrusive way, their legs touching at the knee. Jean and Jules and Josh and Suzie sat across from them.

Josh was smiling broadly as he leaned over and slapped Billy on the knee. "Man, we kicked *ass* tonight." In addition to Billy's wins, Josh's other artists—Luke Bryan, Darius Rucker, Keith Urban, and Lady Antebellum—had all scored big over the course of the three-hour awards show. "You guys did me proud."

As the car filled with endless chatter about the evening, Ian looked around and realized that, apart from Billy's family back in New Orleans, these were the people he loved most in this world, and they were all here supporting him and Billy. Ian's mind drifted back to how he'd almost screwed it all up and lost Billy in the process.

Within the first year of his and Billy's relationship, Ian had broken it off because of his own insecurities and the leftover pain and betrayal he carried around with him from his first and only other relationship. But Billy wouldn't hear of it. After Ian had reluctantly explained what had happened, Billy had decided things didn't add up, so he'd gone in search of Todd Slocum, Ian's first love. After Billy found him, it didn't take them long to realize Todd and Ian had been played by their parents because of their conservative Christian values. They'd led Ian and Todd to believe each had betrayed the other in order to keep them apart.

Ian looked over at Billy and a smile formed on his lips. Billy was very animated as his hands flew through the air, apparently describing something from earlier in the evening he thought was funny.

God I love that man! And to think I came so close to losing him. Not once, but twice.

The first time was when Ian's own insecurities drove a wedge between him and Billy. The second was at the hands of Buck Stevens, a crazed and jealous ranch hand.

Late one evening, Buck had tricked Billy into driving out to the ranch by telling him Jules had been hurt. But when Billy had arrived, Buck had knocked him out with a baseball bat, dragged him to an old cabin on the ranch, tied him to a bed, and set the cabin on fire. Ian and Todd, as well as Jules and Jean, had gotten there barely in time to save him. But unfortunately Buck had already fled the scene and had never been apprehended. For a year after the attack Ian was always looking over his shoulder, expecting Buck to come back and finish the job. *It all seems like eons ago.*

The limo pulled up to Sambuca and came to a stop. Billy reached over, squeezed Ian's knee, and grinned. Ian winked and straightened Billy's tie as Billy's bodyguard opened the limo door. "You ready, boss?" Butch asked.

"As ready as I'll ever be, Butch. Let's do this."

Butch stepped aside and cameras again flashed from every direction. "Go," Ian said. "Your fans are waiting. We're right behind you."

Billy stepped over him and exited the limo to hundreds of screaming fans. He patiently signed autographs and took selfies all the way up to the front door, stopping one last time and waving before they all disappeared into the restaurant.

The group was immediately led to their table, and Billy was bombarded with people congratulating him all along the way. Throughout the first part of the night, he posed for pictures with the other Capitol artists, as well as the label execs, and it was about midnight before he finally got to sit down and join his friends.

"MAN!" BILLY said, slipping into the large semicircular booth, joining Jules and Josh. "Where is everyone?" he asked.

Jules and Josh simultaneously pointed to the dance floor.

Billy turned in the direction they were pointing and burst into laughter. Ian, Jean, and Suzie were in the middle of a large crowd line dancing to Travis Tritt's "I Smell T–R–O–U–B–L–E."

"I don't think I've ever seen Ian move so fast," Billy said.

"I think he learned to dance like that when he worked at the saloon," Jules said. "And he's pretty good at it."

"Damn straight," Billy agreed. "And the girls aren't too bad either."

Jules shook his head and let out a chuckle. "All I know is I'll bet my wife is going to need the heating pad tonight."

Josh and Billy roared with laughter.

Jules winked. "The ole girl still has it, though."

"She certainly does," Josh agreed.

When the girls and Ian returned to the table, they slid into the booth out of breath and fanning themselves. "Jesus," Jean said. "I'm too old for this."

"Not a chance," Suzie said. "And Ian? I can't believe you've been holding out on me all these years."

Ian smiled. "Not holding out. It's called self-preservation."

Suzie smacked him on the arm. "Since the cat is out of the bag and I know you're a closet dancer, we've got a lot of catching up to do."

"Exactly what I was trying to avoid," Ian said, rolling his eyes.

"You better save me a spot on your dance card for when we get home," Billy whispered to Ian.

"Always," Ian promised.

The DJ cranked up George Strait, and Suzie took Ian by the hand and led him to the dance floor, while Jean did the same to Jules, leaving Josh and Billy alone at the table.

"Shall we?" Billy asked, holding his hand out to Josh.

"Do you lead or follow?" Josh asked, then quickly covered his ears. "No! On second thought, I don't think I want to know the answer."

Billy laughed as Josh smacked his hand away.

Josh looked out at the dance floor and found Suzie and Ian. "I know Ian's going to get me for this," he said, "but as long as he's dancing with Suzie, I'm off the hook."

Billy laughed again.

"By the way," Josh said, "you did really well tonight."

"Thanks, man."

"You know what this means, right?" Josh asked.

Billy wasn't sure what he was talking about. "I'm not sure."

"You can pretty much write your own ticket with the label now," Josh explained. "You've been a great moneymaker. You've stayed out of trouble and delivered exactly what was expected of you and more."

Billy thought about what Josh was saying. "Can I ask you something?"

"Sure," Josh said.

Billy looked around and leaned in closer to Josh. "I'm tired of living in the closet, Josh. What do you think the label would say if I... we... came out?"

"Whoa, Nelly!" Josh whispered.

Billy raised an eyebrow. "Nelly? Is that a gay joke?"

Josh's face turned red. "No! But you're right, bad choice of words. Sorry. You know I'm new at all this gay stuff."

"All this gay stuff?" Billy repeated.

"Oh, hell. You know what I'm talking about. But...," Josh added, "that's not what I meant about writing your own ticket with the label, Billy."

"I know it's not, but after everything Ian and I had to go through to finally be together, it sucks to have to constantly sneak around. I mean... we can never be ourselves when we're in public, and it blows the big one sometimes."

"'Blows the big one'? What a lovely term," Josh said. "Is that a gay term?"

9

Billy laughed. "Nope. Just another bad choice of words."

"So I guess we're even, then," Josh teased.

"Yep."

"So, back to coming out," Josh said. "Nashville and country music are about as homophobic as it gets, so I don't think the label would be happy about your coming out."

"But what could they do?" Billy asked.

"I'm not quite sure, but I do know there is a little thing called a contract. And it has a behavioral clause in it, and I think your coming out, in their eyes, might be a behavioral issue and could be considered cause for termination."

"Would they do that?"

"I don't know, but I certainly don't want to find out," Josh whispered.

"Maybe it would be better to go ahead and do it and then beg forgiveness from the label afterwards?"

"I don't think I would go that route," Josh suggested. "Are you really serious about this, Billy?"

"Man, you sound like Ian," Billy said. "He feels the same way."

"Then if you won't listen to me, Billy, listen to your partner—or manager, whichever hat you want him to wear at the time—and think long and hard before you make any decisions."

"Enough with the innuendoes," Billy teased. "Long and hard? Really?"

Josh blushed again. "I swear, you gays turn everything into innuendoes."

Billy chuckled. "But seriously, Josh," he said, "let me ask you a question. What was the first thing you did when you and Keith won your CMA for collaborating on his latest single?"

Josh didn't answer and looked like he was reliving the moment. And then it all seemed to make sense. Josh hung his head and mumbled, "I kissed Suzie."

"Exactly," Billy said. "But I wasn't able to kiss Ian." Billy pointed to the dance floor. "Your wife is out there dancing with my partner, but if you wanted to dance with her, you could break in. But if I wanted to dance with Ian, and I sure as hell do, I can't. Do you see my point now?"

Josh frowned. "I do, Billy, I get it. Look, I think everyone should be free to love whomever they choose. I don't get what all the hoopla is about, but unless you're willing to chance your career for your relationship, I'd give this a lot of thought."

Billy nodded. "I have, and I will continue to until I find a way to make it work for all parties. But thanks for listening."

Josh rested a hand on Billy's shoulder. "Any time. And I'll tell you what I'll do."

Billy cocked his head to the side.

"I'll do a little behind the scenes investigating to see if anything like this has ever happened at Capitol and see how they handled it. If they didn't terminate a contract, then a precedent might be set, which could help if you did decide to make a move and it got ugly."

"Thank you, Josh. I knew you'd understand."

Before Josh could answer, Ian and Suzie bounced up, followed by Jean and Jules.

"You got yourself quite the little dancer," Ian told Josh. "She's all but worn me out." Ian slid in next to Billy and leaned in close. "But don't worry, I saved one more for you."

Billy reached under the table and squeezed Ian's knee.

"Me too," Ian whispered.

IT WAS not quite 4:00 a.m. when the limo pulled up in front of their town house.

"Congratulations, Billy," Buster said as he closed their limo door.

"Thanks, man," Billy replied. "And thanks for all you do for me. I'm lucky to have you in my organization."

"Happy to be here," Buster said. "And hey? When are you gonna get a place of your own and stop mooching off Ian?"

"Hell, I don't know," Billy said. "I'm always on the road, so it's one less thing I have to worry about. And besides… it seems like a waste of good money to pay for a house that'll sit empty most of the time while I'm away. Maybe one day, though."

Ian breathed a sigh of relief at Billy's quick thinking. "Hey, Buster, what the fuck?" he said, looking back over his shoulder as he walked up the front steps. "What are trying to do? Break me? I rely on his rental income."

"Oh shit! You guys are too funny," Buster said, laughing. "Have a good night, guys."

As Ian unlocked the front door, he heard Billy's voice. "Drive safely."

Ian laid his tuxedo coat and bow tie over the banister and pulled his boots off and dropped them in the foyer. He walked into the den, plugged his phone into his stereo, and opened iTunes. He queued up the song he'd downloaded in the limo and set his phone down on the hearth.

Billy turned the deadbolt with an audible click, and Ian sighed. *Behind closed doors. Finally!*

When Billy walked into the den, Ian took him by the hand and led him to the couch. He slid Billy's tuxedo coat over his shoulders and let it fall to the floor. He pushed Billy down to the couch and sat in front of him on the ottoman. He untied Billy's bow tie and let it hang around his neck as he released the top button of Billy's shirt. One of Billy's boots was next, and he cradled Billy's foot in his lap and rubbed it for a few minutes before reaching for the other.

When Ian was done massaging Billy's feet, he got up, walked over to his phone, and pressed the play button. The intro started for Rascal Flats singing "Bless the Broken Road."

Billy grinned broadly. "You remembered our song."

"You mean... the song you sang at Jean's shortly after we started dating."

"The song I sang to *you*," Billy added. "It fit so perfectly."

Ian nodded. "And still does. More so now, I think."

He offered his hand to Billy, and when Billy took it, Ian pulled him up onto his socked feet and brought him in close. "I've been waiting for this moment all night."

Five years hadn't dampened his attraction to his cowboy. Every time they were this close, Ian's heart still threatened to beat right out of his chest.

"Me too," Billy said, leaning down and covering Ian's lips with his own. When Billy's tongue slipped into Ian's opened mouth, Ian's heart rate increased yet again. By the time the kiss finally ended, they were both breathless.

"I'm so proud of you, Cowboy," Ian murmured. "And I love you so much."

"I love you too, Ian. None of this would have been possible without you. I'll never be able to find enough ways to thank you. But I swear I'll die trying."

"I'll start making a list," Ian teased. "Now, I promised I'd save you a dance. Dance with me, dammit."

Ian put his left hand in Billy's right and took the lead position. He slid his other hand around to the small of Billy's back and brought him in closer.

"You're gonna lead and everything?" Billy asked.

"It's your night off, Billy Boy. I'm doing all the work."

Billy pulled back and looked Ian in the eyes. "All the work?"

Ian nodded and drew Billy in again. "All the work," he whispered. "Now move with me."

And Billy did. They swayed slowly to the music, Billy following Ian's lead. Eventually Ian dropped his left hand and slid it behind Billy's back, resting it on Billy's ass. Billy wrapped both arms around Ian's neck, ran his fingers through Ian's hair, his breath heavy on Ian's neck. Damn if Billy's gentle touch didn't go straight to Ian's crotch. The combination of Billy in his arms and Billy's groin grinding against his had Ian's erection pressing against the inside of his tuxedo pants.

When the song ended, Ian rose up on his tiptoes and kissed Billy gently. "Let's go upstairs."

Billy smiled down at him as Ian took him by the hand and led him through the hall and up the stairs. When they reached the bedroom, Billy started unbuttoning his own shirt, and Ian slapped his hands away. "Me" was all he said.

Ian finished undoing Billy's shirt and slid the bow tie out from under his collar. He moved to Billy's wrists and removed his cufflinks one at a time. Then he slipped Billy's shirt over his shoulders. Next Ian released Billy's pants. They fell to the floor, and Billy stepped out of them. Ian led him to the bed, eased him down, and knelt in front of him as he removed Billy's socks.

Standing in front of Billy, Ian slowly and seductively undressed while Billy's eyes bored into his. When he was down to his underwear, he maneuvered Billy onto his back and climbed on top of him. Ian crushed his lips against Billy's desperately, needing to be as close as he could possibly get.

Ian slid down and straddled Billy's knees. He ran his hands gently over Billy's tight abs, needing to feel his warm skin. He pulled Billy's underwear down and hooked them under Billy's balls, exposing his erection. Ian then ran his tongue up and down Billy's length several times and then moved lower, to his balls, taking them one by one into his mouth and sucking gently.

Billy trembled beneath him, letting the smallest of whimpers escape his lips. Ian pulled Billy's underwear completely off, and Billy opened his legs, allowing Ian access to every part of him. Ian slid his hands under Billy's ass and raised him off the bed a little as he took Billy's length into his mouth.

Billy gasped as Ian swallowed him down to the back of his throat and then slid back up again. Ian fisted Billy's erection and moved his hand up and down in unison with his mouth. Billy's breathing increased, and Ian gripped the sheets under them. Suddenly Billy's hands were running through Ian's hair and guiding his head up and down. With each stroke of Ian's mouth, Billy's head and shoulders rose off the bed and then down again as he arched his back. Ian moved lower yet and ran his tongue over the little patch of skin between Billy's balls and opening. Billy raised his knees, giving Ian more access, and Ian took advantage of the opportunity. He grabbed the back of Billy's thighs and pushed his legs back, then ran his tongue over the area continuously until Billy was gyrating under him. Ian spread Billy's cheeks apart and teased his opening with his tongue, getting it ready for what was coming next. When Billy was covered in saliva, Ian licked his finger and slipped it inside. Billy gasped again and pushed against the invasion.

Ian moved his finger around until Billy cried out in pleasure. He instinctively honed in on the spot that always brought Billy to the verge of sharing his load much too quickly. Ian leaned forward and licked the head of Billy's leaking cock, tasting a sample of Billy's juices that made him hungry for more. He took Billy into his mouth again and sucked in unison with his finger penetrating Billy's opening.

"You," Billy screamed. "Now!"

Ian pulled off and chuckled. "What a bossy bottom you are."

"Now, Ian," Billy cried out again.

Billy reached into the nightstand drawer and threw a bottle of lube at Ian, hitting him in the chest. "A *dangerous* and bossy bottom," Ian teased.

He coated his length in lube and rubbed more over Billy's opening. He positioned himself and pushed in gently. Billy cried out again, and Ian stopped.

"Don't stop!" Billy said. "Move."

Ian pushed all the way in until he was at Billy's core. Warmth surrounded every inch of his length, and Billy tightened and pulsed around him as he took himself in hand and stroked. Ian slapped his hand away and repeated, "Me. All me."

Billy put both hands behind his head and offered Ian a seductive smile, gazing at him with so much desire, Ian thought he might lose his load right then. He gave Billy a minute to adjust and then started moving, slowly at first. He slid almost all the way out, held there for a second, and then plunged all the way back in again.

"Jesus!" Billy hissed, fisting the sheets and arching his back.

Ian rode the waves of desire flowing through him with each and every thrust, and every time Billy cried out, Ian got closer and closer to his release.

Ian took Billy's length in hand and pumped it in time with his thrusts, picking up the pace. They were now slapping against each other so hard Billy's head was bent against the headboard. But he didn't seem to care. He was obviously there for the ride, and Ian didn't want to disappoint.

"Now, Ian, I'm—oh Jesus!" Billy screamed.

Billy tightened around Ian as he shot his load, the first spurt landing on his chin. Ian kept pumping, and Billy released the rest of his load on his chest and abs.

As Billy shuddered under him, Ian felt his release building. The first signs of orgasm started to course through him, and he instinctively picked up his pace again.

Billy was still taking it like a man, and when Ian's balls tightened, he filled Billy with his release.

"Billy!" Ian called. "Oh God, Billy."

Billy gripped the backs of Ian's thighs and pulled Ian against him. Hard.

Ian's orgasm seemed to last forever, and Billy was still holding his own. Ian finally slowed until he collapsed on top of Billy. They lay still. Ian didn't want to move as they panted and attempted to catch their breath, and Billy made no objection until Ian finally began to pull out.

"No," Billy whispered as Ian slipped from him. "Not. Ready."

Ian slid off of Billy and lay on his back. Billy rested his head on Ian's chest, and Ian took Billy into his arms and held him tightly as they lay in the afterglow of their lovemaking.

Sometime later Ian slipped from the bed and returned with a warm cloth. He cleaned Billy and himself and then tossed the cloth to the floor. When he crawled back in bed and snuggled up behind his sleepy lover, Billy took his arm and pulled it against his chest. "I love you, Ian. Thank you."

"I love you too, Cowboy. And congratulations again."

Chapter Two

IAN WOKE to the sound of a cell phone ringing. He reached behind him and ran his hand over the surface of his bedside table. *Where is the damn phone?* Ian looked over his shoulder, but his phone wasn't anywhere in sight. He sat up and realized the sound was coming from the floor, from Billy's tuxedo pants to be exact. *That's Billy's phone?* He looked back at Billy, who was sleeping soundly, and didn't have the heart to wake him. *Shit!*

Ian glanced at the clock. *Seven thirty in the morning! Who in the hell is calling at this hour?*

He slipped out of bed, fished through Billy's pants pocket for the cell, and stared at the caller ID. *Josh.*

"This better be good," Ian whispered into the phone, walking into the bathroom and closing the door behind him.

"Where in the hell are you? I've been calling you for an hour."

"My phone didn't ring." *Oh shit!* Ian suddenly remembered he'd left his cell phone on the hearth in the den. "I left my phone downstairs. Sorry. What's wrong?"

"We've got trouble."

"What kind of trouble?"

"Have you seen the papers or been on the Internet this morning?"

"Josh," Ian said with a frustrated tone in his voice. "We only got home a few hours ago. No. We haven't seen anything. Why?"

"Billy's all over it," Josh explained. "And not in a good way."

"All over what?"

"Wake up," Josh said in a harsh tone. "The news!"

Ian peeked through the door and looked at Billy, who appeared to still be sleeping. "Hold on," Ian said as he slipped out of the bathroom, through the bedroom, and headed downstairs. "What's going on?"

"Just get to your computer and go the *National Intruder's* web site."

"The *National Intruder*?" Ian asked as he slipped in behind his desk and started typing on his keyboard.

When the home page popped up on his computer screen, Ian's heart sank to his knees, and he suddenly felt nauseous. On the front page of the tabloid magazine was a picture of him and Billy locked in an embrace when Billy won the Entertainer of the Year Award. Ian's face was buried in Billy's neck, and the camera must have clicked at the moment Ian kissed him there. The caption read, "Billy Eagan shares an embrace with his secret lover!"

"Holy fuck," Ian said in disbelief.

"Holy fuck is right," Josh repeated.

"Josh, you know how careful Billy and I are. This was a split second in time."

"Well, that split second was caught on camera. And that's not the half of it," Josh said. "I hate to tell you this, but it gets worse."

"Jesus!" Ian hissed. "How much worse?"

"Read the story and call me back."

Ian clicked the "complete story here" button and the scene that unfolded in front of him almost took his breath away. Josh had been right.

There were various red-carpet shots of him and Billy together, arms draped over each other's shoulders or around each other's waists, as well as shots of them embracing whenever Billy won an award. More pictures of them together at Fan Fair and shots of them at Billy's many personal appearances. But the worst was a picture taken last night, and Ian remembered the exact moment it was taken. It was a shot of them at the table, staring at one another endearingly, and it showed Billy's hand resting on Ian's leg under the table. "How in the fuck did a photographer get that shot? He must have been on the floor across the room."

By themselves, each of the photos, except for the under-the-table shot, could have been manager and artist celebrating a win or posing for a camera, but all of them taken together painted a very different picture. Ian started to read the article.

IN A bombshell world exclusive, the *National Intruder* rips the lid off country superstar Billy Eagan's secret gay lifestyle. A lifestyle that, now exposed, could certainly threaten his livelihood and perhaps ultimately force his career to crash and burn.

The thirty-three-year-old singer made national headlines as he soared up the country music charts with his first number-one hit, "The Love of A Man," which he claimed was about his mother and father's marriage from his mother's perspective. But an anonymous source says, "The song was always about his manager and lover, Ian Dillon." The source goes on to say, "The *real* Billy Eagan has blatantly lied to his adoring fans and his record label about his sexuality from the get-go."

Eagan and Dillon met five years ago when Dillon was scouting talent for Capitol Records and discovered Eagan, who'd recently won an open-mic contest at the popular Jean's Magnolia Saloon in Nashville. Capitol signed him to the label shortly thereafter, and Eagan's been with them ever since. Our source says, "There was an instant attraction between the two, and Eagan even sang a song directly to Dillon one night at the same club."

Our own independent investigation revealed Eagan was married for a short time in his youth but was divorced for irreconcilable differences before the age of twenty-two. His former wife was unavailable for comment. But since arriving on the Nashville scene some five years ago, Eagan has never had a serious relationship, at least with a woman. Not so much as a casual girlfriend. The same goes for Ian Dillon, Eagan's manager and alleged lover. Astonishingly, sources say it was Eagan who pursued Dillon, going so far as to locate and invite a former lover of Dillon's to Nashville as part of a ploy to convince Dillon to take a chance on him.

By all accounts the two men are inseparable. "You see one and you see the other," our source tells us, also revealing, despite Billy's massive fortune, he still shares Dillon's small Westhaven townhouse about an hour outside of Nashville. They apparently travel together exclusively and always share hotel rooms. Our source confirmed he once witnessed Billy and Ian making out like teenagers. "Eagan is outright lying to everyone about being a homosexual, and when his fans read this, he'll be considered the George Michael of country music."

Eagan almost died a little over four years ago along with struggling country singer Tina Roth, allegedly at the hands of her estranged boyfriend, who attempted to burn them to death. And guess who saved the day? If you guessed Dillon, you are correct. According to police reports at the time, Dillon—along with Todd Slocum, Dillon's aforementioned ex-lover, and local businessman Jules James, owner of the Lazy H Ranch where the incident occurred—showed up on the scene, and Dillon charged into the burning building, risking his own life for Eagan's. The perpetrator was never found and is still at large.

Eagan has achieved great success. He has released sixteen platinum singles and four platinum albums, won multiple awards, and continues to tour almost nonstop. His dedication to his fans is undeniable, as is theirs to him, but can his success continue now that his fans know the truth about Billy Eagan? All that remains to be seen.

We attempted to reach Capitol Records for comment, but no one returned our e-mails or phone calls.

"HOLY JESUS," Ian said to himself. "Who in the hell is their source?"

Ian dialed Josh back on the house phone. When he heard Josh's voice, he launched into a tirade. "Those fucking assholes! This is gonna kill Billy's career! They timed this perfectly to coincide with the CMAs! And what fucking anonymous source?" he asked, out of breath but still trying to keep his voice down and not wake Billy.

"Who the hell knows?" Josh replied. "At first I thought it was all speculation, but there are too many facts."

"What facts?" Ian asked. "'The Love of A Man' was not written for me. That song was written long before we met."

"What about Todd?"

"What about him?" Ian asked incredulously.

"Could he be the source?"

"No!" Ian snapped. "Todd wouldn't do something like that. He and Luke are two of our best friends and the only people we've shared our lives with except for Billy's family back in New Orleans, Jean and Jules, and you and Suzie."

"Okay, fine," Josh said. "But who else knew Billy tracked Todd down?"

"Jean and Jules and you and Suzie. That's it. As far as I know."

"I guess it really doesn't matter who the source is," Josh admitted. "We have to come up with a plan and release a statement, and we need to get Billy a hidden-away girlfriend and get him married pronto."

"Married?" Ian questioned.

A sound at the office door made Ian looked up. Billy was standing in the doorway, wearing nothing but his underwear and rubbing his eyes. "Who's getting married?" he asked.

"Billy's here, Josh. I'll call you back."

"Morning," Billy said in a sleepy voice. "What are you doing up at this hour?"

"I got an early morning call from Josh," Ian said, having trouble looking Billy in the eye.

"About what?"

He's gonna have to see it sometime. No use trying to keep it from him. God! This is breaking my heart.

"This!" Ian said clicking back to the cover of the tabloid and turning his laptop around.

BILLY GAZED at Ian's laptop, blinked a few times, and smiled. "Nice picture. Is that from last night?"

"Yes."

"Who took it?" Billy asked.

21

"We don't know," Ian said, sounding apologetic. "This is all my fault, Billy. I'm so sorry."

Billy felt like he was in some sort of a fog. "What's your fault? What are you sorry about?"

"Read the headline," Ian said.

Billy looked at the screen. "Billy Eagan Shares an Embrace with his Secret Lover!" Confused, he pulled the laptop closer to him and squinted at it. "What is this?" he asked.

"It's the cover of the *National Intruder*."

"What?"

Billy dropped into a chair in front of Ian's desk and clicked on the story. He scanned the pictures of him and Ian, his eyes widening as he realized what he was looking at. "We've been *outed*," he mumbled.

"Yeah," Ian said, a frown consuming his face. He stood and started pacing behind his desk.

While Ian paced, Billy read the article. When he was finished, he closed Ian's laptop and sat back in his chair, fingers linked and resting on his bare stomach.

Billy closed his eyes and sorted through the barrage of emotions running through his head. Sympathy for Ian topped his list, followed by surprise, fear, betrayal, and anger. But when they all ebbed, the one emotion that stayed with him was simple relief.

"We've been *outed*," he repeated.

"Don't worry about anything, Billy," Ian said, his frown growing deeper. He stopped pacing, rested his hands on the back of his desk chair, and stared at Billy. "Josh and I will work with your publicist to prepare a statement. We'll set up press interviews and you'll do the morning talk-show circuit and explain it all away. It'll all be fine. It worked for Randy Travis and Kenny Chesney. We'll make it work for you."

A lightbulb went off in Billy's head and things started to make sense. He sighed as he realized why the word "married" was being bandied about. Billy opened one eye and gazed at Ian. "You and Josh think you're marrying me off?"

"Billy. As much as it pains me," Ian admitted, "it might be the only way."

"You'd let me marry someone else?" Billy asked, his heart full.

"Of course I would," Ian said, a worried expression on his face. "I would do anything for you."

He would do that for me.

Billy stood, walked around Ian's desk, and took Ian into his arms. "Don't worry. I'm not marrying anyone but you. And we're not preparing a statement of denial either."

"What? Billy! It's the only way to save your career," Ian said, breaking out of their embrace. He threw his hands up. "Look at Ty Herndon. He had numerous number-one hits, and he lost his record deal simply because someone accused him of being gay. And what about Billy Gilman? Once rumors started surfacing about his sexuality, he couldn't even get a record deal. Nashville is not ready for this, Billy. They're gonna crush you."

Billy sighed and pulled Ian back into his arms. "I don't care whether Nashville is ready or not. This is our lives, and I'm not going to go on television and publicly deny you and what we have."

"But—"

"No buts," Billy said covering Ian's lips in a quick kiss. "Do you love me?"

"You know I do," Ian replied.

"Are you ashamed of our love?"

"Hell no!" he said without hesitation. "I love you, and *I* don't care who knows it. But this is not about me."

"Are you afraid of losing your job?"

"Of course not!" Ian huffed. "I'm not under contract, so if they fire me, it would be a clear-cut case of discrimination. But… I don't care about *my* job. I am afraid of you losing your career."

"I don't care about my career—I mean, I do," Billy corrected, "but not at the expense of our relationship. Again, I'm not going to lie about you and me. I won't do it."

"Come on, Billy. I know you love what you do."

"I do love it, but I do not need it. There's a difference. And I'm not to the point where I'm willing to denounce you or marry

23

someone I don't love to keep doing it. All I really care about is you and me. Nashville may turn their back on us, but I guarantee you the world will not. And if they do, we sail off into the sunset and reap the benefits of all the hard work we've put into this. And hell! At the worst, we take a few years off and spend some of our money. These things have a way of blowing over. Who knows? Maybe one day Nashville will come around."

Ian's shoulders slumped, and he hung his head. He looked so defeated; Billy's heart ached for him. *He thinks this is his fault. How do I make him understand?*

Billy lifted Ian's chin with his forefinger until their eyes met. "We both knew our relationship was going to come out sooner or later because I plan on being with you for the rest of my life. I'm not going to prove this article right and lie about this now, and then when it all does come out say I was too scared and confused to be honest. That's not who I am. And you know that."

Ian closed his eyes and sighed.

"Look at me," Billy said.

Ian opened his eyes.

"You know me better than anyone," Billy said, "and you know I could never live with myself if I lied about this."

"What if I ask you to do it for me?" Ian asked.

Billy contemplated his answer and then sighed. "For you I would do it," he confessed and meant it. "But I would hate myself. Is that what you want? Come on, Ian. Do you really want to live the rest of our lives in the closet?"

Ian didn't answer.

Billy pulled Ian to him. "I know this is all new to you," he whispered in his ear, "but I've been thinking about it for a long time now. And my mind is made up."

Ian stepped back, ran his fingers through his hair, and started pacing again. "But you'll be throwing away everything you've— we've—worked for."

"Ian? Is this about me losing my career, or is this about you?"

Ian stopped in his tracks and looked at Billy, the pain obvious on his face. Billy immediately regretted the words, but it was too late. It was on the table, and deep down he knew the answer, but he needed to hear Ian say it.

"How can you ask me that question?" Ian asked through gritted teeth. "Of course it's about you. Everything I do is for you. Always."

"Then do something for you, for us. And in the end, you'll still be doing something for me. Like always."

Ian started pacing again.

"The way I see it," Billy said, taking Ian by the shoulders and stopping him again, "I may very well lose my career, but we'll gain so much more. So you'll know this is not a quick decision, I had a conversation with Josh about this last night while you guys were on the dance floor."

"Oh Jesus," Ian said. "You talked to Josh about this?"

"Yeah! And he said everything you're saying to me right now."

"I figured as much," Ian confessed. "This isn't going to be easy for him either. The fact that he knew about us and didn't tell the label."

"None of this is going to be easy on any of us," Billy agreed. "But *everything* worth *anything* in life never is."

"The label is gonna hold Josh responsible for this, you know," Ian said.

"Then we'll tell them Josh knew nothing about our relationship. That way he's off the hook completely."

"But Billy…," Ian pleaded, tears filling his eyes, "I don't want you giving up your career for me."

"I'm not doing this for you," Billy explained. "I'm doing this for me, for us. I love you, Ian, and I'm not going to lie about that. To anyone."

"But—"

"Again with the buts, Ian. Stop it! You—" He kissed Ian lightly on the lips. "—and I—" He kissed him again, a little deeper this time. "—are going public with our relationship—" And a little deeper still. "—record label or no record label." And with that… one last crushing kiss. "Now let's get Josh on the phone and come up with a plan for the best way to do that."

Ian sighed and laid his forehead against Billy's chin. "Are you sure?"

Billy kissed Ian again. "I've never been more sure about anything except for the way I feel about you. Are you with me?"

"Always," Ian said. "You know whatever your decision, I'll be right by your side as always."

"JOSH! I know all that," Billy said. He had Josh on speakerphone. So far it wasn't going well. "I just heard the same sermon from Ian. And although I know you both have my best interest at heart, you're not hearing me. This is ultimately *my* career and mine and Ian's life. In the beginning I went along with keeping our relationship on the down low, but now that it's out, I won't lie about it."

Billy looked up, and Ian recognized the "please help me" expression on his face.

"Josh," Ian said calmly. "You know Billy. He has more integrity in his little finger than most men have in their entire body, and I get why he won't lie. He's made up his mind. Trust me on that."

"What do you mean *he's made up his mind*?" Josh asked sarcastically. "I think you've both lost your fucking minds. That's what I think."

"Maybe so," Ian agreed, reaching for Billy's hand. "But if this is what Billy wants, I'm behind him one hundred percent."

"It's not only your hides on the line here," Josh said. "What about the position this puts me in with the label?"

"We've already thought about that, and we're prepared to tell the label you knew nothing about our relationship. You can act as surprised, shocked, and pissed off as you want, and we won't take it personally."

"Thanks a lot," Josh said. "And wouldn't that win me a gold medal in the friendship Olympics?"

"It's okay, Josh," Billy said. "We know you care about us, but neither one of us wants your job on the line over this."

"Come on," Josh pleaded. "You know I don't give a fuck about who sleeps with whom, but this is not me. This is Nashville."

"I'm sorry, Josh, but our minds are made up," Billy said. "And as soon as I hang up with you, I'm calling Mike's office to set up a meeting with him, the heads of promotion, media and public relations, and you and Ian, of course. So you should expect a call from Mike with a date and time. But just know, we're gonna do this with or without your and the label's support."

"So you're simply going to call the president and CEO of Capitol Records Nashville and tell him you're a big ole homo and you and Ian have been secretly playing *hide the salami* for the last five years, and you didn't think the label needed to know?" Josh asked.

"Well, not exactly. But something like that," Billy said. "I'm sure Mike has seen the *National Intruder* by now, like we have, so it shouldn't come as too much of a shock to him."

"Of course he's seen it," Josh confirmed. "Who do you think woke me up at six o'clock this morning? I didn't answer and let it go to voice mail, but I've been dodging calls from him all morning waiting to talk to you two before I called him back." Josh sighed. "I wish you would reconsider, Billy."

"I know you do, Josh, but this is our life, and I'm not going to lie about it, for all the reasons I've already explained to you."

"You know this is probably going to get ugly," Josh said.

"Probably," Billy said. "But it certainly doesn't have to."

"And so you'll be prepared," Josh explained, "in my opinion this is what is going to happen. The label will calmly try and talk you into denying everything. They'll remove Ian as your manager, make you buy your own house, find you a suitable wife, and get you married ASAP. Or, if you don't agree to their plan, they'll threaten to, and possibly will, terminate your contract, citing the airtight behavioral clause. Or lastly, and probably the most damaging to your career, they'll keep you under contract and simply halt all promotions, rendering you dead in the water. You don't perform. You don't make any personal appearances. You don't record. You simply exist in limbo until your contract expires, therefore killing your momentum and ultimately your career."

"First of all," Billy said, "my contract is up for renewal in seven months. They can terminate it or they can freeze me out all they want. Ian and I can use a long vacation. Or...," Billy continued, "I can explain everything to Mike like I explained it to you. We can come up with a mutually beneficial media and press plan, and we can make this all go away with a positive spin on it."

"And what do you think the chances of that happening are?" Josh asked.

"I think it depends on how persuasive I am," Billy said. "I mean... it's pretty plain and simple. If we deny, the press will keep digging and eventually out us anyway. If we come clean, there is no story, and the entire thing goes away. By doing absolutely nothing, the label could actually come out smelling like a rose and be the first in Nashville to set a precedent and take a step into the twenty-first century."

"And if they still don't see it your way?" Josh asked.

"Then Ian and I take our case to the courts and, more importantly, the court of public opinion. This is 2015, Josh. Times have changed. Same-sex marriage is legal in thirty-five states. People are tired of fighting about discriminating against gay rights and want to move on to something else.

"We'll do the morning-show circuit and then hit the late-night circuit and go to every radio station that'll have us. One way or the other, we won't sit back and accept anything less than we deserve as good, morally responsible people. I have no problem going public with what the label intends to do to me and us."

Through the speakerphone, Josh's finger tapping lightly on his desk, a habit Ian knew Josh had when he was thinking hard about something, was clearly audible. "Okay," Josh said. "I'll make you a deal."

"We're listening," Billy said.

"If you're hell-bent on doing this your way," Josh said, "I'll go to bat for you with the label."

"You would do—"

"Wait," Josh interrupted. "I'm not finished."

"Okay, sorry! Go on, Josh," Ian said.

"Guys, this is my livelihood," Josh explained. "And I can't help anyone if I lose my job, so you'll have to stick to your original plan and back me up on the fact that I didn't know anything about the relationship. I hate going that route, but if Mike thought I intentionally kept this information from him, knowing it might impact the label, he'd be furious, and he would have every right to be."

Ian looked at Billy and nodded. Billy nodded back. "Absolutely! We've already agreed to that," they both said in unison. "What else?"

"Only this," Josh said. "It's important to me you know I never really thought of you guys as anything other than Ian and Billy. I mean, I knew you were gay and in a relationship, and I know it sounds silly, but you're just you."

"That's the way it's supposed to be, Josh," Billy said. "I don't look at you and Suzie and picture you having sex or even think of you in those terms. Ian and I know you're married and do all those things, but you two are just you as well. Sort of a unit, like Ian and me."

"Okay, so that's it," Josh said. "In my opinion, that's the only thing they can fire me for. And if we stick to our plan, then my job should be secure."

"Done," Ian said.

"Now, I'm not making any promises," Josh clarified. "This is all new territory for me, and we know how the labels in general have handled this type of thing in the past. But I promise you I will do my best to make this work out for everyone."

Ian took Billy's hand again and gave it a squeeze. "I don't know how we'll ever repay you, Josh."

"Oh, I'll come up with something. Trust me."

"You've always been a great friend to both of us," Billy said. "But this is more than we could have hoped for. As far as we're concerned, you've already won the gold medal in the friendship Olympics."

"All right, guys," Josh said. "Let me handle it from here and see where Mike's head is. You two lay low, and I'll be in touch shortly."

"Will do," Billy agreed. "And… thank you again, Josh."

"Save it," Josh said. "We still have a huge mountain to climb."

A LITTLE over two hours and fifty calls—from various news outlets, radio stations, and television shows (all wanting comments about the cover of the *Intruder*)—later, Billy saw Josh's name on Ian's caller ID.

"Ian!" Billy yelled. "It's Josh."

Ian joined Billy in the den and they sat side by side on the couch as Billy put the call on speaker. "Josh?" Billy said. "Tell us you have some good news."

"I wish I could," Josh said. "Mike was completely blindsided and is fuming about the story. He's threatening to sue the *Intruder*, and of course we can't let that happen because he'd certainly lose."

"Did he ask if the story was true or not?" Ian asked.

"No," Josh said. "I don't think he's prepared for the answer. But I did tell him I was as shocked as he was when I saw the article. I'm setting the stage for when he does ask."

Ian looked at Billy. "We got it," he said. "What did Mike say to that?"

"Shit," Josh said.

"*Shit* what?"

"He said 'Shit!' You asked what he said. He said 'Shit!'"

Ian laughed nervously. "Josh, we've been bombarded with calls from the press, so I know the label must be getting bombarded as well. What are they saying?"

"Right now the formal statement is 'no comment,'" Josh said. "But tomorrow will be a different story, depending on how this all turns out."

"So now what?"

"Mike summoned us all to his office at ten o'clock sharp tomorrow morning."

"Oh Jesus," Ian said. "That's not good."

"What do you mean 'not good'?" Billy asked. "It's exactly the chance I was hoping for. I'll make him understand. I promise both of you."

"I hope so for all our sakes," Josh said.

"Anything else?" Ian asked.

"That's all I have for now."

"Will you call us if you hear anything?"

Josh chuckled nervously. "You know I will. And Billy?"

"Yeah?"

"You better bring your A game tomorrow."

HOURS AFTER they'd gone to bed, Ian lay there staring up at the ceiling, listening to Billy's slow, steady breathing. *How can he be so fucking calm when his entire career is hanging in the balance?*

Ian kept going over every possible outcome of their meeting tomorrow. Scenarios spun in his head, and he couldn't shut them down. He knew the encounter would either cement or ruin Billy's career, and the unknown scared the shit out of him. And then there was Josh. His career was also on the line. If he lost his job, it would be purely because of Ian and Billy.

Unable to take it any longer, Ian slipped out of bed, tiptoed into the bathroom, peed, and, after washing his hands, stared at his reflection in the gold-framed mirror over the sink. *I look like crap.*

He looked tired, worried, and stressed, which made sense because that's the way he truly felt. There were deep circles under his eyes that hadn't been there yesterday, and his cheeks looked sunken in. Even his skin looked white and pasty, giving him a ghastly glow. He patted his face and pinched his cheeks and nothing changed. Finally giving up on doing anything about his appearance, he slipped into his bathrobe and made his way downstairs.

He peeked through the gathered sheers in the sidelights of the front door and, as there had been all day, there were still news trucks stationed on the curb outside their townhouse. *Don't these shits ever go home?*

31

He walked into the kitchen and opened the refrigerator door, squinting against the intrusion of bright light in the darkness of the downstairs. He reviewed its contents and nothing appealed to him, so he closed the door and leaned against it, feeling exhausted. He rubbed his eyes and face and then ran his hand through his hair. *Jesus Ian. You've got to get it together before tomorrow.*

But how?

Tomorrow could be the beginning of the end for Billy.

Oh God, I need a drink.

Ian poured himself a glass of cabernet, hoping the alcohol might help him unwind a little and maybe, just maybe, allow him to sleep. He sat on the couch and listened to the rhythm of the pendulum as it swung below the clock hanging on the den wall. *Tick. Tick. Tick. Tick.* The sound was deafening. He went over to the entertainment center and popped Billy's latest CD into the player. He paced back and forth, sipping his wine, and within seconds Billy's smooth, soulful voice came over the speakers. The sound instantly calmed him and he swayed to Billy's voice.

When the first song ended and the next one started, Ian sat down on the couch again, and the tension in his neck and shoulders began to ease. As his head cleared, it became more and more obvious to him their plan for tomorrow was a big mistake. In his opinion, Mike was not going to go for the whole "we never hid anything" approach, but Billy was dead set on this and Ian had to support him. The only people he'd talked to all day were Billy and Josh, and somehow Billy had convinced them both to jump on the bandwagon with him. But now in the wee hours of the morning, it all seemed so hopeless.

I need a voice of reason.

Galvanized, Ian picked up the phone and dialed.

"Ian. Is everything all right, honey?"

Just hearing Jean's soft voice made him feel instantly better. She and Jules had been the first people he'd opened up to when he'd arrived in Nashville a broken man. She had taken him in, given him a job at the saloon, and she was the one who'd jump-started his career in the music business. She was like the mother he never had, and somehow he knew she would make him feel better.

"I hope it's not too late, doll?" Ian asked.

"Not at all," Jean replied. "I'm just closing down the saloon. But you didn't answer my question. Is everything all right?"

"You mean you haven't heard?"

"Heard what?" Jean asked with a nervous tone in her voice.

"It's all over the tabloids," Ian said.

"After the awards show, Jules and I slept most of the day, had a quiet dinner at home, and then we drove to the saloon to check on things. We haven't seen the papers or even watched television. Ian, you're starting to scare me."

Ian told her about the tabloid cover and then waited.

"Ian, I'm so sorry," Jean said. "Of course we hadn't heard or we would have called. How is Billy holding up?"

"Oh, he's sleeping upstairs like a baby. I'm the one who's falling apart."

"Honey, Jules and I can be there in an hour. Just let me close everything up here."

"No!" Ian said. "No need for that, I just wanted to hear your voice."

"So what are you going to do about all this?" Jean asked.

Ian told Jean about Billy's plan.

Jean sighed into the phone. "His thought process is technically right, but we both know how Nashville deals with homosexuality."

"They simply don't," Ian replied.

"Exactly. But on the other hand," Jean went on, "in just the last year, I've seen a slight sea change. With Chely, Ty, and Billy Gilman coming out in 2014 and making some noticeable headlines, it's bringing a lot of unwanted attention to the homophobia that's alive and well in Nashville."

"But Jean, it's not the right time," Ian said. "Things may be starting to change, but Nashville is nowhere near accepting gays and lesbians as country music artists."

"Ian, you've got to support Billy in this," Jean explained in a soft tone. "In the end it's his career, and if he's tired of living in the

33

closet, so tired that he's willing to possibly give it all up, he must really want this."

"He says he wants it badly," Ian confirmed.

"Then I think you have your answer," Jean said. "Besides, if Nashville won't accept Billy with open arms, there are many other places that will. Honey, Billy is a big star with very loyal fans, and they won't turn their backs on him. I just know it."

"I hope you're right."

"He loves you, Ian. He's tired of hiding it, and I can't blame him."

"I'm tired of hiding too, but not so tired that I'm willing to risk Billy's career."

"That's just it, Ian. It's Billy's career," Jean reiterated, "and it sounds like he's making it pretty clear what's most important to him. I know things may change for you too, but—"

"I'm not at all worried about me," Ian interrupted. "I love my job, but if it's over tomorrow, I'll do something else."

"It won't be over," Jean reassured him. "You'll just keep right on managing Billy's career whether it's with Capitol or not. When does Billy's contract expire?"

"Seven months," Ian said.

"Oh, Ian," Jean said. "That's no time at all. The label may try and convince you both that if Billy doesn't do what they want him to do they'll derail his career, but in my opinion seven months is not long enough to do that. Look at Garth Brooks. He's been out of the spotlight for over a decade and the public still wants him back. Now more than ever."

"What do you think the label will do?" Ian asked.

"Who knows," Jean said. "Probably demand he marry some made-up woman he's been secretly seeing for years. But I know the record business pretty well, and a star of Billy's caliber doesn't just fade away so quickly. My gut instinct is that the label won't throw away one of their top five artists over this. They may bitch and moan and try and scare the hell out of both of you, but in the end, I don't think they'll make a bad business decision over a moral issue, especially one that people are finally beginning to see *isn't* a moral issue to begin with."

Ian sighed, feeling like a weight had been lifted off him. "Thank you, Jean."

"Oh, honey. No need to thank me. Are you sure you don't want us to come over there?"

"I'm sure. Besides, Billy's sound asleep upstairs, and I don't want to wake him."

"Too late."

Ian looked over his shoulder. Billy was standing in the hall leaning against the wall.

"Jean, Billy's awake, so let me hang up. I can't thank you enough for talking me down."

"I love you, and tell Billy I love him too. Please call me after the meeting tomorrow."

"Will do," Ian said. "Good night, Jean."

"Good night, honey. Now get some sleep."

"Okay. Bye now."

Billy walked over to the couch and sat next to Ian. "You okay?"

"Yeah. I'm sorry if I woke you."

"You didn't, technically. I woke up and you weren't there, so I came to look for you. Talk to me, Ian. Tell me what's got you up at this hour."

"I just needed to make sure we weren't making a big mistake."

"So what did Jean say?" Billy asked.

"Well, to be honest, I figured I'd call her for a little emotional support, and she'd side with Josh and me and together we would find a way to make you change your mind."

"And?" Billy asked.

"Damned if she didn't side with you. Sort of."

Billy shook his head. "God, I love her. Tell me what she said."

"Basically she said she didn't think the label would make a bad business decision because of a moral issue, and she thought you would be fine whatever way the label went."

"And that's it?" Billy asked.

"Mostly," Ian said. He relayed the rest of the conversation to Billy and then downed the last of his wine.

Billy took Ian's hand. "Do you feel better now?"

"I do."

"Then that's all that matters. Just know that whatever happens tomorrow, we will be fine."

Ian smiled. "I know. I'm just scared for you."

"I know you are, and I love you all the more for it, but I'm so happy we're doing this. I can hardly wait to be able to claim you in front of the world."

"If you're happy, then I'm happy."

Billy kissed Ian on the lips. "Thank you. Do you think you can sleep now?"

"I think so," Ian replied.

"Then let's go back to bed."

Chapter Three

AT NINE forty-five the next morning, Ian and Billy walked through the doors to the Capitol building. Billy had anticipated some stares and maybe a few whispers, but to his surprise, everyone had been as friendly and cordial as they always were when he was in the building.

They were escorted to the private conference room of Mike Dungan, the president and CEO of the Nashville division of Capitol Records, and found Josh already there and looking over some paperwork.

When Josh saw them through the walls of the glass-enclosed room, he stood and met them at the door. "Morning guys."

"Morning," Ian and Billy said in unison.

"Mike will be in at ten, but he wanted some time alone with you before the rest of the participants joined the meeting at eleven."

"The rest of the *participants*?" Billy asked.

"Mainly public relations and marketing," Josh confirmed. "He wants to see how they plan on making this all go away."

Billy cast a glance at Ian, who seemed to be masking his stress fairly well, at least on the outside. He was a little pale and had the thinnest sheen of perspiration covering his forehead, but all in all, he was holding it together fairly well. Billy knew him inside and out and was certain he was scared shitless.

"At least we know what we're up against," Billy said, pulling out Ian's chair.

They all took their seats, and Billy watched as Ian linked his fingers together and rested his hands on the table in front of him.

Billy tapped the table with his forefinger to offer a little reassurance and support. Ian looked at him and smiled weakly.

37

Scotty Cade

Billy, on the other hand, was calm, cool, and collected. He was ready for this. He'd been dreaming of the day when he and Ian could be themselves in public, and he had no doubt he was going to convince Mike to support them by speaking from the heart. Not because he was acting or had rehearsed his speech, but because he was talking about him and Ian. His speech couldn't be anything but heartfelt. He hoped Mike Dungan saw it the same way.

When Mike entered the room, they all stood and exchanged formal greetings. Billy, Ian, and Josh took their seats again, and Mike sat at the head of the table.

"So, boys?" Mike asked, looking at Billy and Ian over his glasses. "Anything you want to tell me about what came to light on that godforsaken *National Intruder* cover?"

"Yes, sir," Billy said.

"First of all, is it true?" Mike asked.

Billy looked Mike in the eye. "Most of it is true."

"I see," Mike said. "So there's still hope. Please tell me the part about you being in a relationship with your manager is the part that's not true." He paused and looked at Ian.

"I'm sorry, but I can't do that, sir," Billy replied.

"Fuck!" Mike shouted, slamming his fist on the table. "Then just for shits and giggles, what is it that's not true?"

"The part about 'The Love of A Man' being written for Ian."

Mike raised an eyebrow. "Well, thanks for fucking clarifying that."

"Sir!" Billy said. "That song was written two years before I met Ian, and it *was* about my mother and father."

Mike looked back and forth between Billy and Ian, "And you took it upon yourself to keep this little tidbit from me?"

"No, sir. Not intentionally," Billy said. "It's never been an issue. We didn't lie about it, and although we tried to keep it on the down low, we never really kept it from anyone."

"That's bullshit, Billy, and you know it." Mike turned to Josh. "Did you know about this?"

"Mike," Josh said honestly, "I was as shocked as you are when I saw the story."

38

Billy silently applauded Josh. He'd phrased his answer so he wasn't actually lying, but he'd led Mike to believe he didn't know.

Mike looked at his watch and then looked at Billy. "You fellas have a little under an hour to convince me why I shouldn't fire Ian on the spot for inappropriate behavior and terminate your contract immediately."

"Well," Billy started, "firstly, because I'm good at what I do, and because I'm one of the top five producing artists in Nashville. I will make music, Mike. If you terminate my contract, it won't be for Capitol, but I guarantee you *I will make music.*

"Secondly...." Billy went on to cover every heartfelt reason he'd used to persuade Ian and Josh to support him, with an emphasis on his integrity and the way he tried to live his life.

"So now you've had your say," Mike said, "you're gonna listen to me and do exactly what I say. You're gonna start by moving the hell out of Ian's house and buying one of your own. Next you are both going to deny you are involved in any way, and we're going to find both of you girlfriends, and Billy's story is going to be he's been dating this woman secretly for a long time. And you're going to marry her, Billy. Ian, I could care less if you marry yours, but you'll date her publicly and be seen as much as possible."

Billy stood up and opened his mouth to protest, but Mike waved him off. "Sit down, Eagan. I'm not through."

Billy sat.

"And furthermore, if you don't do what I say, I will halt your career where you sit. I'll tie you up in court so long that by the time we either settle or your contract expires, your career will be over."

Billy's blood was boiling up from his toes, and at some point soon he was going to explode. "Enough!" he yelled. "Mike! We will do nothing of the sort. You want to play hardball. Fine, let's play hardball. My contract is up in seven months. You want to terminate our agreement and/or freeze my career, you go right ahead. I can sure as hell use a seven-month vacation. But understand, you will not stop Ian and me. Or my career. And you want to fire Ian, go ahead. We have more money than we can spend in our lifetime, so he doesn't need your job."

39

Billy stopped and took a deep breath. His heart was racing, and he couldn't believe he was saying these things. But once he opened his mouth, it all came flying out. "Now Mike," Billy continued, "if you want to work together and find a solution we're all happy with, I'll be glad to do it, but I will not lie or deny my relationship with Ian. It's going to come out eventually, and if I allow you to cover this up now, we will never again have the ability to say we didn't lie about it. If we come clean, we can truly say we never lied to anyone, nor did we ever try to mislead or cover it up."

Billy looked around the room and studied Ian's, Josh's, and Mike's faces. Ian and Josh were both white as sheets, and Mike's face was bloodred. He was wearing a look somewhere between anger and shock. The man looked like he was going to blow one way or the other at any minute.

"I've not had a girlfriend since my divorce, and that was over ten years ago, so they can't say I used random women to hide my sexuality. Secondly, Ian and I have appeared at every event together for the last five years. You, Josh, nor anyone else thought anything of it. So they can't say we kept our life hidden. And thirdly, all we need to say is we are extremely private people and never talked about it publicly.

"Mike, it's kind of like when a baby falls down and bumps its head. If you scream in fear and run over to the child, the child is gonna start screaming as well. If you don't make a big deal about it, the baby won't. I really believe this is all that simple."

To Mike's credit, he seemed to be calming down. He was listening to Billy's rationale, but Billy knew it wasn't going to be this easy. "You say you have a label to protect. So how are you protecting your label by terminating one of your top five producers? Think about everything I've said, Mike. For once, don't go into panic mode and react. Just think about it."

Mike didn't respond, but Billy could tell the wheels were turning, so he kept going. "We only get one chance to take this stand," he said. "If we allow you to cover this up and deny, Ian and I will be running from it for the rest of lives. And when it comes out, we will be the ones coined liars. I'm sorry, but I can't allow you to do that."

Mike leaned back in his chair and sighed deeply.

"If you refuse to see this my way, you leave me with only a few options," Mike finally said. "One, I follow your request and go public with your relationship, we see where the chips fall, and if it gets ugly, I terminate your contract and send you on your way. Two, I simply terminate your contract now, save us all the hassle, and you can come out to the heavens if you want. Or three, I keep you here under contract and stop promoting you, therefore leaving your career dead in the water."

"Personally, I vote for one," Billy said.

"I'll bet you do," Mike replied sarcastically. Mike looked at Ian. "Is this some long-term thing that's worth risking this man's career over, or is this some fly-by-night experimentation?"

Billy sat back, and although he was pretty sure he knew what Ian was going to say, he really wanted to hear it.

"Mike," Ian said, "Billy and I have been together exclusively for the last five years. We love each other very much, and this is as real as it gets. I wouldn't risk his career if I wasn't one hundred percent sure about our longevity."

"Billy?" Mike asked. "Do you feel the same way as Ian does?"

Billy sat up and squared his shoulders. "I absolutely do."

Ian continued. "Mike, neither Billy nor I took the decision lightly. And of course my loyalties lie with Billy, but please know I put my personal feelings aside and wore my Capitol hat above all else. And I did everything I could to try and change Billy's mind. And Josh did the same. Neither of us made this decision easy on him."

Billy interjected. "Ian is telling the truth. He and Josh were relentless about the label and my career, first and foremost."

Mike was quiet for a long time. When he finally spoke, it was to Billy. "How do you think your fans will react to this news?"

"Well," Billy said, "I think the women will react the same way they would have if I was caught in a secret relationship with a woman. The gay men are gonna say 'I knew it.' And the straight men... I don't really know how they're gonna react."

41

"I'll tell you how I think they're gonna react," Mike said. "They're gonna stop buying your records." He glared at Billy silently as if daring him to deny it.

Billy felt compelled to fill the silence. "I'm sorry, but I don't agree. I know my fans, and they are extremely supportive. Women make up eighty percent of my demographic, but besides that, nowadays there are gay bull riders, gay NASCAR drivers, gay pop stars, and gay men protecting our freedom in the military. Why can't there be gay country singers?"

"That's a good question, son," Mike said. "And to be completely honest, I don't have a definitive answer. I think it has something to do with the fact that we live in the Bible belt. There are cowboys, rednecks, and men's men everywhere we turn. Not to mention the old country music demographics. But... I'm not a dinosaur. I know the world is changing right before our eyes, and regardless of my personal feelings on the matter, I've got a record label to run and protect. As you say, you're one of my top five producers, and if we kill your career, we all lose. On the other hand, if we support you, we take a greater risk of collateral damage."

Billy cleared his throat. "Mike, can I ask you a question?"

Mike nodded.

"I've been with your label for almost five years. During that time have I, or Ian, for that matter, ever been in the tabloids? Have we ever acted irresponsibly with the press? Gone to rehab? Embarrassed the label in any way or acted anything less than professional?"

"No."

"Then why would you think all of a sudden we're gonna start making out in public? This doesn't change anything regarding our work ethic or our professional persona. Sir, with all due respect, we've been walking down red carpets together for the last five years, and no one has suspected we were anything more than best friends, or an artist and his manager. We're private people, Ian and me. So private that, in spite of all of our public appearances, we've been able to keep our relationship out of the public eye for the last five years. That's got to say something."

42

Mike linked his fingers behind his head and looked up at the ceiling. "Billy, I have to admit you talk a good game. If we deny, I see where we keep digging ourselves into a hole, but if we admit yes, the story's over, but we're gonna take some heat and lose some fans."

"But I think we'll also pick some up," Josh interrupted. "Mike, with Ty Herndon and Billy Gilman publicly coming out recently and shedding light on Nashville's homophobia, I think this is a great opportunity for Nashville and Capitol to move forward with the rest of the world and do the right thing. The support for those guys has been overwhelming. And what about this new guy, Steve Grande? He's openly gay and his songs and videos have all been going viral.

"We all think we can put a really good spin on this, for the label and for Billy. For starters, we'll have Ian and Billy appear in public as much as possible to show people they'll see nothing but the same two guys they've always seen. They'll do a lot of press and explain to the world what they just explained to us. They love each other, and they've never lied about that."

During Josh's speech, Billy glanced at Ian, and the same feeling of pride he was experiencing was plastered all over Ian's face. *Josh has always been there for us. Why would I think he'd abandon us now?*

Mike was still looking up at the ceiling. Without moving, he simply said, "I'll tell you what. Let's get PR in here and see what kind of spin we can put on the whole damn thing. I agree it's time Nashville steps up to the plate and takes a stand."

Billy couldn't believe his ears. Was it going to be this easy?

He looked at Ian, who was smiling from ear to ear, and Josh was doing the same. He and Ian had a shot at making this work. They actually had a real shot.

BILLY, IAN, and Josh took an active role in the meeting as Mike and the public relations team sat down and brainstormed how to spin the story. Ian was having a hard time believing what was actually happening. Not only had Billy convinced Mike to not terminate his

43

contract, but together, he and Josh had convinced him to take a stand, albeit a little one, against homophobia in Nashville. The label was going to support Billy, and that was more than Ian could have ever asked for.

Three hours later, everyone agreed Billy's suggested spin was the one that worked best. They wouldn't cover it up; they would face it head on with the label's support. After all, it was the truth, and the truth was always the best approach.

As the meeting moved on, the PR department simultaneously started on the press release and the scheduling of as many personal appearances as time would allow. Tomorrow morning Billy, Ian, and Josh were scheduled to fly to New York, and the next day Billy and Ian would start appearing on the East Coast morning-show circuit, starting with *Good Morning America, LIVE with Kelly and Michael, The View*, and whatever else they could squeeze in. Then they would take a break and start all over again with the late-night shows, including *The Tonight Show with Jimmy Fallon, Late Night with David Letterman, The Daily Show with Jon Stewart*, and *Last Call with Carson Daly*.

The next morning they would get back on the plane and fly directly to Los Angeles to do *The Talk, The Ellen DeGeneres Show, Conan, Jimmy Kimmel*, and *The Late Late Show with Craig Ferguson*. And while they were on the West Coast, they would hit the two major country stations the next morning and then start making their way back to Nashville. They would crisscross the country doing interviews with all the country radio stations in the major markets. Ian knew it was an aggressive schedule, but they needed to get the momentum going and make everyone see that Billy was still Billy.

When the meeting finally adjourned, Ian was mentally, physically, and emotionally exhausted. If the look on Josh's face meant anything, he was feeling the same way. But Billy seemed to be on cloud nine. They walked to the elevator together, and Ian noticed Billy was almost floating on air, he was so happy. When the elevator doors opened, they all stepped inside, and when the doors closed again, the three of them ended up in a bear hug lasting almost to the ground floor.

When the elevator doors opened again, they were all appropriately in their corners, and they stepped into the hall and walked calmly out of the building.

Once outside, Josh offered Billy and Ian high fives. "I can't believe we did this, guys," he said. "This is unheard of in Nashville."

"It's time," Billy said. "And I'm glad Ian and I are the poster children for Homos in Nashville."

Josh laughed. "Ian, how do you feel about all of this?"

"I'm ecstatic," he replied slapping Billy on his back and squeezing. "I must say I'm a little nervous about all these personal appearances. I mean... I'm always *behind* the camera and *back*stage, not front and center."

"Don't you worry," Billy said. "I'll be right there with you."

"You'll do fine," Josh reassured Ian. "Both of you will. Now you guys get home and get packed, and I'll do the same. I'll see you tomorrow morning at the airport."

The entire ride home, Billy was like a kid. His excitement caused Ian to forget about how exhausted he really was.

"We did it. We actually did it" was all Billy kept saying.

"It was all you, Billy," Ian said. "Josh and I supported you, but it was all you. You spoke so eloquently about our relationship and our commitment to each other; I couldn't love you any more or be any more proud of you than I am right now."

"We're a team, Ian. You and me," Billy said. "And together we can do anything we put our minds to. We're gonna change Nashville, Ian. I can feel it."

When they pulled into the garage, Ian watched as Billy got out of the car, walked around to the driver's side, and stared at him through the window with such a look of desire it took Ian's breath away. When the large garage door closed behind them, Ian's door was open, and Billy guided him out of the car, then shoved him against the garage wall and covered his lips in a crushing kiss. Ian was suddenly moving and being kissed at the same time. Billy kissed him all the way up the garage stairs, started undressing him on the way down the hall, and sat him on the stairs as he removed his boots and socks, pulled his shirt over his head, and then pulled off his pants. He dragged Ian to his feet and kissed him all the way up the stairs to their bedroom. When they reached the bedroom, Ian found himself backed up to the bed and pushed down to land solidly on his back. He looked up as Billy stripped down to his underwear and climbed onto the bed, landing on top of Ian.

BILLY GROUND his crotch into Ian's and could feel Ian's excitement as their bulges pressed against each other's. He caressed every part of Ian's body without breaking their passionate kisses. He couldn't believe they would no longer have to hide their love for each other. He wanted Ian so badly now, he could barely control himself.

Billy moved his mouth to Ian's neck as he ran his hand down the outside of Ian's arm and held his hand tight. Then he released his hold and rubbed farther down, to Ian's thigh and back up again. Ian's warm fingers lightly stroked his back, which sent a chill down his spine. Ian tilted his head into the soft, moist lips teasing and biting at his neck while wrapping his legs around Billy's lower thighs. He reached down with both hands and pulled on the waistband of Billy's underwear, letting Billy know he wanted them off. He released his legs from behind Billy's back and gently guided Billy up to his knees. Ian slid Billy's Calvin Kleins down to his knees, and as Billy rolled to his side, using his toes, Ian pulled the underwear the rest of the way down to Billy's ankles. Billy, in one quick move, finished the job and then reciprocated, sliding Ian's underwear down and off.

Billy wanted this to last forever; he wouldn't hurry, not this time, no matter how much he wanted Ian. He would tease and torment him until he was about to explode with passion. And then, and only then, would he allow Ian the release he was so desperate to achieve. Still lying alongside Ian, Billy fondled the sensitive skin around Ian's pulsing erection. He lightly ran his fingers through Ian's pubic hair, never once touching his rock-hard dick. Ian was still on his back with his head turned, watching Billy intently. Billy rolled his head ever so slowly, and his eyes met Ian's. Ian found his mouth again and kissed him hard. Billy continued to gently tease Ian's sensitive areas, and Ian raised his right knee as a silent invitation for Billy to explore at will. Billy reacted by lightly brushing his fingers over Ian's inner thigh and slowly making his way down to Ian's balls.

Playfully, Billy tousled Ian's balls, gently rolling them through his fingers as he felt them tighten with anticipation. Ian responded with a sound both ravenous and willing, which gave Billy all the encouragement he needed to continue his exploration.

After releasing Ian's balls, Billy slowly ran his fingers down along the narrow piece of skin to Ian's opening. Ian pulled his mouth away from Billy's and whispered, "I need you inside of me." Billy sensed the urgency of his admission and felt him tremble with anticipation. "I've never before needed or wanted you more than I do right now. I want you, Billy, need you."

Billy rolled back on top of Ian and straddled his upper thighs. He kissed Ian again and then licked his way from Ian's chin down to his left nipple, circled and teased it with his tongue, then licked his way to the other and did the same. Next he continued down past Ian's belly button to the hairs above his dick. He circled the base of Ian's cock with his tongue, which made it jump with arousal.

Want you, Ian. Want you so bad. Never wanted you more.

The litany of his desire played through Billy's head on repeat as he kissed the tip of Ian's dick, making Ian gasp, and hooked his arms under Ian's legs and lifted them over his head. Billy pulled Ian's asscheeks apart, and when his tongue touched the soft pink skin surrounding Ian's opening, Ian trembled and moaned with pleasure. Billy ran his tongue around the edges of Ian's opening and gently tantalized the tender area before pulling his cheeks farther apart and probing inside with his tongue. Ian relaxed his muscles and opened to Billy's warm advances. His breathing was becoming more erratic, which told Billy he was doing his job and doing it well.

Billy withdrew his tongue and with one fingertip, circled and massaged the tight opening. Billy needed to feel the warmth of Ian's insides. He opened the drawer and grabbed the lube, fumbled the cap up, and spread the thick gel around Ian's opening. Slowly, he slipped his index finger inside. Ian moaned as his cock jumped and twitched in response. The intimacy of Ian totally giving himself to Billy in this way was always so overwhelming, but this time it felt different. Like the first time.

Ian had always given Billy everything, emotionally and physically, but now Billy craved an even deeper bond. It left him feeling somewhat vulnerable and exposed, but at the same time warm, safe, and connected. He trusted Ian, and Ian had always seemed to know exactly what he needed. Billy opened up to the feelings and let them consume him.

He was immediately brought back into the moment by the look on Ian's face as Billy teased and fingerfucked him. Ian closed his eyes and threw his head back as he said, "Oh God, Billy, you feel so good."

"You haven't really had me yet. But you will soon," Billy promised. He took the head of Ian's dick into his mouth as Ian cried out and tightened around his finger. "I'm going to give you everything I have." Ian inhaled as Billy trembled. Billy was sure he was shaking in anticipation of the pleasure to come.

"Yes," Ian moaned, his ass wiggling as Billy slipped in a second finger and fucked him slowly. "I want you, Billy. I need you now." Ian fumbled until he found Billy's cock and squeezed and kneaded it like dough.

Billy was now quivering as the look of desire on Ian's face overtook him. His hips began to thrust forward into Ian's tight grip around his cock.

"I want you so badly, Billy," Ian begged. "I need to feel you inside me. Please, fuck me now."

Billy slowly eased his fingers out of Ian, kissing the head of his dick. He again opened the flip-top of the lube bottle and squeezed some into his hand. He made sure Ian was adequately lubricated and spread more along the shaft of his own erect cock. As aroused as they both were, Billy was determined to take it slowly, at least at first. When Billy positioned the head of his dick at Ian's opening and applied pressure, Ian tensed up slightly. Billy began to push inside him—a little at first, a pause for Ian to adjust, and then a little more. After several minutes of gently invading Ian's ass, Billy was in all the way. Billy paused, and their eyes met. "Are you okay?"

Ian smiled reassuringly, and Billy relaxed and began to slowly pull out and ease back in with a smooth, long stroke, repeating it until he was deep inside again.

Billy bent over and kissed Ian while reaching between them to stroke Ian's erection. Ian's hands gripped his thighs, moving back and forth with each thrust, urging him on.

"God, you feel so good," Ian moaned.

Billy placed Ian's legs over his shoulders and started to fuck him slowly, never breaking eye contact.

Ian arched beneath Billy and groaned with each thrust, moving with Billy and pulling him deeper. "God. God, Billy."

Billy pushed in again. "Fuck, yes," Ian gasped.

Need you, Ian. More. Want more.

Ian's ass was tight and warm and still more perfect than anything Billy had ever felt before. He pulled all the way out this time. Ian looked like he was about to protest when Billy drove back in with one long stroke until his pubic hairs were smashed against Ian's hot ass. Ian whimpered in ecstasy.

"Oh my God, Billy." Ian was trembling, his cock leaking onto his stomach.

Continuing to fuck Ian with strong, deep strokes, which drew groans from each of them, Billy slid his hand free and curled his fingers around Ian's cock.

Ian shuddered and groaned, rocking his hips to meet the next thrust. "God…. Billy, don't let go, please, I'm so close…."

Ian's body moved as one with Billy's, pushing and pulling Billy with every stroke. Billy's fingers were still wrapped around Ian's hot cock, working it with the same ruthless speed with which he was pushing into Ian.

"Oh Ian, yes…." Billy's balls drew up in anticipation of his release, the moment before he came apart and nothing else mattered but the need for one more slide into that tight, welcoming heat.

Ian came in Billy's hand so ferociously Billy could do nothing but follow him. He cried out Ian's name, the intensity of his orgasm stronger than anything he'd ever experienced. As the last of his vitality poured out, he collapsed on top of Ian, shuddering and gasping desperately for air.

Ian wrapped his arms around Billy and began to rub his back and shoulders gently. Ian kissed Billy reassuringly, and Billy relaxed against Ian's chest.

"No, don't move," Ian said when Billy started to stir. "I want to stay like this forever."

"I'm not going anywhere, Ian," Billy said. He lifted his head and covered Ian's mouth with his own, kissing him, loving him, and hoping his feelings were being conveyed in the kisses, because he didn't think he could put them into words.

Billy was holding Ian tightly when he eventually slipped out of him. He saw the regret in Ian's eyes at the unavoidable separation, a regret he shared. The trusting way Ian contentedly settled in beside Billy meant more than he could put into words. Ian had come a long way to fully trust Billy's love, and that was something Billy would never take for granted. He knew how hard believing in someone again had been for Ian, but Billy hoped he'd brought Ian love, peace, and security at last.

NEITHER IAN nor Billy had slept much the night before, so they both drifted off almost immediately. A couple of hours later, Ian woke first. He was wrapped in Billy's strong arms and lay there for a few minutes listening to Billy snoring contentedly.

Knowing they had a lot to do before they left, Ian tried to slip out of bed without waking Billy, but Billy tightened his grip. "Where do you think you're going?" he said sleepily.

"We have so much to do," Ian said, kissing the top of Billy head. "I was going to get a head start."

"What time is it?" Billy asked.

Ian twisted his head to get a look at the clock on his bedside table. "Five thirty."

"Just a few more minutes. Pleeeease."

"Okay, a few, but we've got a lot of packing to do," Ian said. "Our new life is starting tomorrow."

Billy raised his head and kissed Ian's cheek. "Are you excited?"

"Excited and nervous, but I'm ready."

"Me too."

IAN AND Billy sat side by side in the greenroom at ABC studios, sipping on hot coffee while Josh conversed with the segment producer about their upcoming interview with Robin Roberts.

Over the course of yesterday's flight and last night's dinner, they had finalized the press release, which had hit the newswire around seven o'clock this morning, and tweaked the talking points they'd give to each interviewer.

When the limo had pulled up to ABC, it was nearly dawn, and Times Square was still lit up like a Christmas tree. Billy smiled to himself as he remembered standing in the middle of Times Square, grabbing Ian and raising their joined hands above their heads. "Here we come, world. Ready or not," he'd whispered.

"Okay," Josh said. "Everything is set. We've got about fifteen minutes until your segment, but the crew will be here momentarily to mic you both."

"You okay?" Billy asked, looking at Ian.

"Yeah. I am," Ian said. "A little nervous but surprisingly… okay."

Billy squeezed Ian's knee. "After the first one, the rest will be a piece of cake. I promise."

Ten minutes later both Ian and Billy were wired with little microphones on their shirts and power packs attached to the backs of their belts under their sport coats.

"Right this way," an assistant producer said as she led Billy and Ian to the set and gave Josh a place in the audience. She got Billy and Ian seated next to each other and explained that right before the break, George Stephanopoulos would announce what was coming up in the next segment, and the camera would switch to them for a brief moment before they cut for the commercial break. "See the red light on top of the camera?" she asked.

Billy and Ian both nodded.

"When it goes live, the red light will turn to green."

Ian and Billy watched as George and Robin, along with Amy Robach, Ginger Zee, Michael Strahan, and Lara Spencer, sat behind the *Good Morning America* news desk, wrapping up the current segment.

"Here we go," Billy said. "Get ready to smile pretty."

"Next up, Robin sits down with country superstar Billy Eagan and his partner/manager Ian Dillon about the *National Intruder* cover outing them as secret lovers."

The camera panned over as planned, and when the red light turned to green, Ian smiled and Billy waved and winked at the camera.

"Three. Two. One," the producer said. "And we're out. Good job, fellas."

Robin came over, introduced herself, and took a seat across from Billy and Ian. She looked over the talking points. "Anything off-limits, gentlemen?"

"I don't think so," Billy replied, glancing at Ian. "Ian? Anything you don't want to talk about?"

"My family," Ian said to Billy and then turned to Robin. "I would prefer not to talk about my family."

"Noted," Robin said.

"Okay, everyone. We're going live in five," the producer said, holding up five fingers and then dropping one. "Four...." And then she simply used her fingers to silently count down: Three. Two. One.

"A couple of days ago," Robin began smoothly, "the *National Intruder* stunned the world by running a cover story outing country superstar Billy Eagan and his manager Ian Dillon as secret lovers. This morning we have Billy and Ian here with us to talk about that explosive cover and give us all the facts. Welcome, gentlemen."

"Thanks for having us," Billy said.

"Good morning," Ian added.

"So Billy?" Robin asked. "Were you shocked when the *National Intruder* ran the story?"

"Yes and no," Billy replied. "What shocked me was not the fact that they referred to Ian and me as lovers, but as *secret* lovers."

"What do you mean?" Robin asked.

"Ian and I have been a couple for just under five years. And it's never been a secret. I mean," Billy continued, "we've never hidden the fact that we are together. Ian and I have walked the red carpet at every awards show together. We've attended every after-party together, been at every Fan Fair together, and pretty much, with the exception of when I'm onstage, if you see one of us, you see the other."

Billy looked over his shoulder as pictures of him and Ian together—arms draped over each other's shoulders, embracing at an event, and standing next to each other—ran across the big screen behind them. "See," he said with a chuckle. "Do we look like we're hiding?"

"Not to me," Robin agreed. "The article also states that your first number-one hit, 'The Love of A Man,' was written for Ian. Is that true?"

With a sideways glance at Ian, Billy shook his head. "I wish I could say yes, but no. That's not true," he said. "I wrote that song when I was still playing the honky-tonks of New Orleans about two years before my big break. And as I've said all along, it was written about my mother's love for my father."

"Ian," Robin inquired, "the article says you guys met when you discovered Billy singing at a popular Nashville saloon."

"That's true," Ian said, looking over at Billy. "Jean James, the owner of Jean's Magnolia Saloon, and I go way back, and she called me and asked if I would stop by and check out Billy's act. She'd said he was the best she'd seen in a long time."

"Aw shucks," Billy said. "I'm sitting right here, guys."

Ian smiled. "Stop it. And you know I'm not teasing you," he said, giving Billy a wink. "And it was the best move I've ever made, personally and professionally."

"Speaking of professionally, Ian," Robin said. "With the recent accusations from Ty Herndon and Billy Gilman that the overwhelmingly homophobic Nashville ruined their careers, how does Capitol Records feel about this so-called outing?"

"They've been great," Ian said. "The fact that they signed Billy five years ago and have supported us ever since shows they are single-handedly trying to change the way Nashville looks at gay artists."

"You both know I'm a huge fan of country music, and I say, 'Good for you, Capitol Records. We have to start somewhere.' Oh and this is interesting," Robin continued. "The *Intruder* says Billy dug up your former lover to help him win you over. Is that true? And why?"

"It actually is true," Ian said, smiling at Billy. "My first and only relationship ended pretty badly and left me seriously gun-shy of any type of relationship. But thanks to Billy looking him up, my ex and I talked for the first time since our breakup and found out there were a lot of outside forces at work trying to keep us apart. But we worked it all out, and, well, here Billy and I are five years later."

"That's great," Robin said. "Good for you guys." She turned to Billy. "And what's this about you almost dying in a fire a few years back?"

"Yeah," Billy said. "There was a crazy guy I used to work with at the Lazy H Ranch. He was riding on the coattails of his girlfriend, who was trying to make it big at the time, and I beat her out in an open mic contest. He was pretty upset about it and tried to stop us both. Luckily Ian and the owner of the ranch, Jules James, showed up in time to save us."

"And I'm sure glad they did."

"Me too," Billy said, slapping Ian's leg.

"And one last thing. What do you say to your fans who feel betrayed and claimed you lied to them all along?"

Billy turned and looked directly into the camera. "My fans mean everything to me," he said. "Ian and I love each other deeply, and I guess by not talking about our relationship publicly, one could say we lied about it. But that was never our intention. We never tried to hide, but we are both very private people and wanted to keep a little something for ourselves. Besides the fact that we tried to keep a little normalcy in our relationship, personally I was somewhat afraid if fans were focused on our relationship, then they wouldn't be focused on the music. I now realize I was selling my fans short, but it's the honest truth. If I hurt any of you by doing that, I—" He looked at Ian. "*We* sincerely apologize."

"All right, guys," Robin said. "We're almost out of time, but thanks so much for sharing your story with us. And congratulations, Billy, on all the CMA awards, especially Entertainer of the Year."

Billy bowed his head. "Thank you, Robin. I appreciate that."

The producer held out five fingers and began silently signaling the countdown to the end of the interview.

"Thanks again," Robin concluded. "Everyone! Billy Eagan and Ian Dillon."

The green light turned to red, and the segment was over.

"And we're out."

Robin stood and hugged both Billy and Ian. "Good job, gentlemen, and by the way, Billy, I love your music. Can I get you to sign a few CDs for some of my charities before you go?"

"Absolutely. It would be my pleasure."

"I hate to run," Robin said, "but I've got to get ready for the next segment. Again, great job."

Josh walked up, slipping his cell phone into his pocket and wearing a huge smile. "You guys did great, and Mike is very pleased, by the way."

Billy looked at Ian. "We did it."

"We did, and I'm so proud of you, Billy. You made all this happen for us."

"*We* made this happen. Together."

"All right," Josh said. "We'll have time for this later. Right now we need to hop into the limo and head to *LIVE with Kelly and Michael* and do it all over again."

Chapter Four

WHEN THEY got back to their suite at the Carlyle Hotel, Ian sat down, rested his head on the back of the couch, closed his eyes, and listened to Josh and Billy discussing the interviews he and Billy had done earlier that morning. Everyone, including Mike, had been pleased with the way it had all gone down. For the morning shows and daytime television, he and Billy had been careful to make sure the adults had known what they were talking about but hopefully had said things in a way the younger watchers wouldn't quite understand.

But the late-night shows were an entirely different ballgame. Since they could get away with being a little more risqué and blunt, they wanted to be prepared by adjusting the talking points, making little innuendos here and there to play on the comedic aspect of the late-night shows. Make a joke out of the entire outing and use the *National Intruder* in their favor.

By the time they had finished, they'd had just enough time to shower and get over to the NBC studios for the four-thirty taping of *The Tonight Show with Jimmy Fallon*. They arrived with a few minutes to spare, Ian in a black suit and tie and Billy in jeans, a gray wool sports jacket, and an open-collared royal blue shirt. They were wired again as they had been that morning and were watching from the greenroom as Jimmy started his monologue. When the monologue was wrapping up, Jimmy started recapping his guests for the night.

"First up," he said, "we have this year's newly crowned CMA Entertainer of the Year, Billy Eagan. Well, I think I need to talk to my writers. 'Crowned' might not be the best choice of words, since he and his partner were just outed by the *National Intruder*. Get it? Queens. Crowned." The audience cheered so loudly Billy, Ian, and Josh could hear them from the greenroom.

"Oh Jesus, now we're queens," Billy said.

"We were always queens, honey," Ian teased, patting Billy's leg. "Just no one ever mentioned it before."

Jimmy went on. "Seriously, it's 2015, people. Why do we still have tabloids outing people. Who really cares who anyone sleeps with?"

The audience again went wild. "I mean... so what if Billy's gay? What does that have to do with the way he sings? Absolutely nothing. That's what. So anyway, Billy and his 'manager'...," Jimmy said, using air quotes, "will be out here to tell us their story. We also have Lady Gaga and Tony Bennett in the house to sing a song from their latest duet album. And although I haven't seen Lady Gaga's outfit yet, I don't smell raw meat, so maybe there's a clause in Tony's contract preventing her from wearing any type of dead animal."

As the audience roared again, Gaga and her entourage filled the greenroom. Ian, Billy, and Josh stood when Gaga walked right up to them. "I'm a big fan, Billy, and I'm very proud of you boys. It's high time all the gay men and women in show business came out of the closet and stood up for gay rights. I mean, really."

"Thank you," Billy said. "We're fans as well."

Gaga looked at Ian and Josh.

"Oh," Billy said. "I'm sorry."

Billy introduced Ian and Josh and then continued, "We were never really in the closet. We just kept our relationship out of the media."

"Either way, the world knows now, and it can only help the cause. Good job."

Gaga turned on her heels, walked toward the craft services table, and started nibbling on vegetables.

Billy turned back to the monitor in time to hear Jimmy say, "And... we'll be right back."

A page came in for him and Ian, and damned if Billy didn't turn the corner and run smack into Tony Bennett. "Oh, sorry, Mr. Bennett. I didn't see you."

"It's okay," Tony said with his usual broad smile. "And call me Tony. You're Billy Eagan, right?"

Surprised that Tony Bennett knew who he was, Billy was almost speechless. "Ye–yes sir."

"I've heard you, kid, and you're real good," Tony said. "And don't worry about this recent shit storm. It'll all blow over. It always does."

"Yes, sir. And thanks."

Tony continued on to the greenroom, but stopped and turned. "Good luck out there."

"Thanks," Billy responded. "My God," he whispered to Ian. "That was Tony Bennett, and he knows who I am."

"Don't be silly, of course he knows who you are."

"Right this way," the page said before Billy could respond. "Stand right here, and as soon as you hear your names, walk around that corner and you'll be on the set. Mr. Eagan, you sit closest to Jimmy."

Since this was being taped, they didn't have to wait while the show went to a commercial break. Seconds later Jimmy said, "Ladies and gentlemen, put your hands together for country superstar Billy Eagan and his partner, Ian Dillon."

Ian and Billy rounded the corner, and as the page had said, there was Jimmy Fallon standing behind his desk. Billy walked right up and shook Jimmy's hand, then stepped aside so Ian could do the same. Billy sat on the couch next to Jimmy's desk as instructed, and Ian sat right next to him.

"Soooo, according to the *National Intruder* you guys are *lovers*," Jimmy said, drawing out the word. "It also says you've been doing the nasty for the last five years and have had the audacity to keep it from me and all your other adoring fans."

Billy laughed. "Well, not exactly," he said, looking between Jimmy and Ian and smiling broadly.

"What part is *not exactly* right?" Jimmy asked, looking at the audience. "Are you not lovers?"

"Oh yeah," Billy said with a wink at Ian. "Look at him. Wouldn't you want to be his lover?"

The audience roared with laughter, and Ian wiggled an eyebrow seductively at Jimmy.

"Well. Yeah, I guess," Jimmy said, seemingly caught off guard. "I mean… if I swung that way," he added, fanning himself with his cue card and blushing. "Hey, I ask the questions around here."

"Oh, sorry," Billy said. "Never mind."

"So, back to my interview," Jimmy said. "You are lovers, but you don't do the nasty?" he asked, making a face at his audience.

"Oh hell yeah," Ian said. "We do the nasty all right."

Thunderous applause from the audience, and Billy smacked Ian on the leg in a teasing fashion. And more laughter followed.

"So the only thing left would be that you didn't keep this from us?"

"Bingo!" Billy said, raising his fist in the air.

"Then why did we have to read about it in the *National Intruder*? I knew it was a lie. Nothing they print is ever the truth."

Billy and Ian both laughed. "In this case, they were mostly right. The absolute truth is that we've never tried to hide it. It's just that we're private people. We didn't talk about it publicly, but we were everywhere together. On every red carpet, Ian was at my side. Every awards show, he was there. Fan Fair, he was there. The only thing we didn't do is shout it from the rooftops."

"And why not?" Jimmy teased.

"The short answer," Billy said, "is because our relationship was the only bit of normalcy we've managed to hold on to in this crazy world in which we live."

"We just wanted to have something of our own," Ian added.

Jimmy turned to the audience and made a face. "Well I think that was all pretty selfish of you."

"I know, and I'm sorry," Billy said, pretending to pout.

"All kidding aside," Jimmy said in a serious tone. "This is no biggie. And who cares who you sleep with? I mean, it's not like you were parading wives and beards all over the place to keep people questioning, like many celebrities still do. And before you ask," Jimmy said to the audience, "they shall remain unnamed."

Billy laughed. "Finally someone is getting our point," he said.

Scotty Cade

"And your record label is behind you?" Jimmy asked. "I've heard some horrible stories coming out of Nashville regarding gay artists."

"Yeah. We've heard the same stories, and I think most of them have been true," Ian said. "But in our case, we've seen none of it. I've been with Capitol Records Nashville for over seven years now, and Billy's been with us for almost five. They are great people back there. Mike Dungan, the president and CEO of Capitol Nashville met with us personally when the *Intruder* story broke, and he assured us we had his full support."

"Wow! That's great, men," Jimmy replied. "What's next, Billy?"

"We have a couple of months before my next tour kicks off in New Orleans," Billy explained, "so as soon as this press stuff is over, we're gonna take a break and head down there to spend time with my family and relax a little before we start the next tour."

"I think I read somewhere that you're from Louisiana, right?" Jimmy asked.

"Born and raised in New Orleans," Billy confirmed.

"I've had a lot of people on the show who spend time down there," Jimmy said. "Brad Pitt and Angelina Jolie, Sandra Bullock, John Goodman, Nicholas Cage, Harry Connick, Jr., and the list goes on and on."

"It's a great city," Ian said. "So much history, not to mention the great food."

"Tell me about it," Jimmy said, patting his stomach. "I've spent time there myself."

"Maybe we'll see you there sometime, then," Billy added.

"Maybe," Jimmy said. "Hey look, it's been great having you, even if you are a couple of homos." He picked up his pen and made a big checkmark on his cue card. "Now I can scratch gays off my list for this week's lineup. You know we're an equal opportunity talk show."

The audience erupted into applause.

"I'll remember that. And it's been our pleasure," Billy replied through a chuckle. "Even if you are a hetero."

60

"Touché!" Jimmy said. "Give it up, everyone, for Billy Eagan and Ian Dillon."

When the segment ended, Jimmy hugged them both. "I hope I didn't offend you in any way?"

"Not at all," Ian said. "If this is the worst we get, we're home free."

"Oh, but look out," Jimmy said. "You still have to do Letterman."

"True," Billy agreed.

Jimmy shook their hands again. "Best of luck to you both."

"Thanks," Billy said. "We appreciate the support."

Ian, Josh, and Billy piled into the limo once again and headed off to the Letterman show. That show went about the same, as did *The Daily Show with Jon Stewart* and *Last Call with Carson Daly*. Then off to the airport again.

THEIR PLANE took off precisely at ten o'clock that evening, which meant they would get to LA a little after one o'clock in the morning, Pacific standard time. They would go straight to their hotel, get a few hours of sleep, and start all over again with the West Coast shows.

After the plane leveled off, Ian stretched out on the couch and closed his eyes while he listened to the usual banter between Billy and Josh. They were having a glass of bourbon and talking about the Fallon show.

Ian smiled when he thought about how proud he was of Billy. Billy had wanted this so badly, and he'd made it happen. He'd even convinced Mike and Capitol Records Nashville that this was a good thing. And that was no easy feat considering how Nashville had handled gay artists in the past.

The funny thing was, over the years, Josh and Ian both had tried to convince Billy to use a beard every now and then at an award show or personal appearance, to keep the rumor mill from taking off, but he'd always refused. In the end, it had turned out to be a blessing. The fact that he and Billy had been photographed

61

together at virtually every one of Billy's appearances, and that neither Billy nor Ian had ever been linked romantically to any woman since he'd been in Nashville, had worked in their favor. Billy's integrity and honesty had once again paid off. *My man only knows one way to live his life, and that's truthfully!*

Ian felt Billy's hand graze lightly over his forehead and brush his hair to the side. He opened one eye and saw the prettiest blue eyes he'd ever seen looking down at him. "Hey, Cowboy."

"I didn't mean to wake you," Billy whispered.

"I wasn't sleeping," Ian said. "Just resting my eyes."

"You did a great job today," Billy said.

Ian lifted his head and kissed Billy gently. "I was just thinking about how proud I am of you. You made all this happen."

He pushed into the back of the couch and patted the space in front of him. "Join me."

Billy lay down with his back to Ian, and Ian wrapped his hand around Billy's waist, pulling him in closer.

"Ian, *we* made all this happen," Billy whispered. "You, Josh, Mike, and me. All of us together."

"Regardless," Ian explained, "the way you live your life openly and honestly, with no regrets, and the way you never look back, has proven to be our saving grace."

"I can't take any credit for that," Billy said. "It's the way I was raised. My father used to say that lies will always catch up with you, but you never have to try and remember the truth. It's always on your side. And so that's how he lives his life and the way I live mine."

"Your father is a wise man," Ian said.

Billy covered Ian's hand with his own and tucked it up under his chin. "Speaking of, I've been thinking."

"Uh-oh," Ian said.

"Stop it," Billy said, smacking Ian's hand. "You know how I always talk about wanting to see my family more?"

"Yeah."

"What do you think about us buying a second home in New Orleans?"

Ian thought about it for a second and realized he liked the idea. He liked Billy's family a lot, and he loved the city. "I think that's a great idea."

"Seriously?" Billy asked.

"Sure. Why not?"

"Thank you," Billy said, craning his neck and kissing Ian lightly on the lips.

"Ah jeez!" Josh yelled, dropping the newspaper to his lap. "Is this what it's going to be like now that you're, how do they say it? Out and proud!"

"Fuck you!" Ian said as Billy flipped Josh off. "Would you prefer it if we had sex right here in front of you?"

Ian saw Josh lift the newspaper in front of his eyes again and peek around the edge. "Never mind," he said. "Carry on."

"We're kidding," Billy said.

"I thought so," Josh admitted. "But just in case you weren't, I wanted to protect my eyes."

"Fucker," Ian said, throwing a magazine at Josh.

"Hey, stop that," Josh barked. "Don't make me call the *National Intruder* and tell them you guys joined the mile-high club right in front of me."

"You wouldn't dare," Billy argued.

"If you two start bumping uglies on this plane, I swear I will."

"Oh, just read your paper," Billy said, looking back to Ian.

"If we ignore him, maybe he'll leave," Ian said.

"I heard that!" Josh replied from behind his paper.

"You were meant to," Ian added, rolling his eyes.

"So where were we?" Billy asked.

Ian squeezed Billy's waist. "I think we were about to buy a house in New Orleans."

"Yay!" Billy said. "We still have a couple of months off before we go back on tour, right?"

"We do."

"And... since the tour kicks off in New Orleans, maybe as soon as this media circus is over, we can fly down, make a vacation out of it, and start looking for the perfect place."

"I don't see why not," Ian agreed. "Where would you want to live? The French Quarter, or maybe the Garden District?"

"I think my first choice would be the Garden District, but I'm open to suggestions. What's your preference?"

"I vote for something along the parade route on or near St. Charles Avenue. That way we can have big Mardi Gras parties."

"Perfect!" Billy said, pumping his fist into the air.

"Maybe we should try to get a little shut-eye before we land," Ian suggested. "It's gonna be a busy next few days."

"I think I'm too excited to sleep," Billy admitted. "But I'll give it a shot."

Both men closed their eyes, and the last sound Ian heard before he dozed off was the familiar whimpers of Billy's gentle snoring.

So much for being too excited to sleep. Ian woke to the sound of the pilot announcing they were starting their initial approach into LAX and would be landing in about thirty minutes. He opened one eye and peeked at Billy, who seemed to still be sleeping, and then looked across the small jet and saw Josh lying on his back on the other couch, fingers linked across his chest, snoring lightly.

I'll give them a few more minutes before I wake them up!

BEING ON *The Talk* Billy likened to his mother Vicki's coffee klatch with her girlfriends. When he was a kid, his mother's stay-at-home girlfriends would come over every morning before they started their chores for the day, have coffee on the front porch, and discuss the topics of the day. Which, he discovered, was exactly like *The Talk.* The hosts were warm and accepting, and one of the hosts, Sara Gilbert, was a lesbian, which made things a little bit easier. They'd told their story again, been cheered and encouraged by the hosts and the audience, and left feeling really good about the entire experience.

The Ellen DeGeneres Show was a great deal different. Not in the sense that it was better, but the entire production had a diverse feel to it. There was an energy the other shows didn't have, and

Billy tried to put his finger on it, but he couldn't quite figure it out. But it was definitely there.

Before the show started taping, Ellen had joined him and Ian in the greenroom, and together they had a blast watching the audience dancing in the aisles. During their interview, Ellen got him and Ian up on their feet. They put Ellen in a Nashville sandwich and danced into a commercial. Everything so far had gone off without a hitch.

Next they headed to the two major country radio stations, where Billy brought his guitar and sang a few songs live, in between discussing the *National Intruder* story and Billy and Ian's relationship. Everywhere they went people were very supportive of him and Ian, as well as Billy's music.

The day had run its course quickly, and before they knew it, it was time to start the late-night shows. *Conan* and *The Jimmy Kimmel Show* were more of the norm, with a couple of risqué jokes here and there, but of all the shows, the craziest of all was *The Late Late Show with Craig Ferguson*. That man was certifiable, and it was fun as hell to do. Craig had teased Ian and Billy unmercifully, and after a few minutes, they'd given it right back to him. Ian and Billy were so tired by then, they'd started to get punchy. Billy had laughed so hard at one point he'd thought he might pee his pants. Craig Ferguson had the worst case of ADHD Billy had ever seen, and it worked well for his type of show. Craig had gone from one topic to the next with no warning, then back to the gay thing, and then on to the next topic. It was a rollercoaster ride of pure entertainment.

By the time the day was over, Billy, Ian, and Josh were physically exhausted, but they'd accomplished their mission, and they all felt really good about how they'd been received.

Chapter Five

BUCK STEVENS paid special attention to the speed limits, driving at or a little above the posted speed, trying not to attract any unwanted attention as he maneuvered the back roads of the northeast Georgia mountains and the Chattahoochee National Forest. His route would take him to Chattanooga and from there straight into Nashville. It was only about two hundred and fifty miles, but the two-lane roads through all the little towns of backwoods America, as well as the ever-changing speed limits, were causing unwanted delays.

Last night he'd stood in his one-room shack in the rural mountain town of Hiawassee, Georgia, fiddling with the aluminum-foil-covered rabbit ears on the top of his black-and-white television. When he finally got a fairly decent picture, he sat down on his dilapidated love seat, put his feet up, twisted the top off a longneck, and stared at the cover of the *National Intruder* while he waited patiently for the interview with Billy Eagan on *The Tonight Show with Jimmy Fallon.*

Buck's mind drifted back four years to when he'd lost a promotion at the Lazy H Ranch because of Billy Eagan. And to add the icing on the cake, Eagan had beat Buck's girlfriend, Tina Roth, in a singing competition, which had really pissed him off because she was going to be his meal ticket. He'd been out of his mind with anger at both of them, and since she was no longer going to be his ride out of the mundane, he'd come up with a plan to do away with them. He'd lured Billy to the ranch, knocked him out, and tied him to a bed next to Tina in an old storage cabin on the ranch and torched the damn thing. He smiled as he remembered the light from the dancing flames filling the evening sky, but then cursed under his breath at how his life had been changed forever. Again because of that asshole Eagan.

After he'd fled the scene, thinking no one would ever know it was he who'd set the fire, he'd heard on his truck radio that Billy and Tina had actually survived the inferno, saved by Billy's faggot boyfriend and his ex-boss. With fingers now pointing directly at him, Buck had been forced to flee Nashville rather hastily to avoid being arrested. Since then his life had been anything but pretty: forced to live in hiding, bouncing from one odd job to another to keep food in his stomach and a roof, however leaky, over his head.

In the process he'd lost about forty pounds, grown a long beard, shaved his head, and stayed mostly out of sight for the first year. He'd done a pretty good job of keeping his anonymity, but he'd never stopped vowing revenge for the many wrongs Billy had done to him. Billy Eagan owed him, and he was going to pay.

Buck had spent years writing letter after letter to every news outlet he could find, trying to get someone to listen to what he had to say about Billy Eagan and his boyfriend, Ian. And finally… the *National Intruder* had called, interviewed him extensively, and agreed to run the story. Buck had been rather proud to be referred to as the "anonymous source" who would finally sink Billy Eagan and his booming career. The story had earned him a whopping ten grand, which was more than enough money to fund his plan to rid the world of the queer singing sensation and finally give him a chance to come out of hiding.

As Buck watched the tail end of the nightly news, he saw a story about a kid who'd been sexually abused by a priest while he was an altar boy and thought back to his life and the things he'd been forced to endure at the hands of his alcoholic mother and a perverted stepfather.

BUCK'S BIOLOGICAL father had been killed in Afghanistan when he was just a baby and his mother, Maggie, had turned *to* alcohol and *away* from him. She'd mentally checked out of any type of productive life, and for the most part, a teenager she'd paid to stay with him had raised him. When he turned six, the girl moved away, and he had to become self-sufficient or starve to death. As far back as he could remember, he'd had to fend for himself as well as take care of his mother.

Month after month Maggie spent all their combined pensions on alcohol, and when they were on the verge of being evicted from their rundown apartment, she took a job as a glorified barmaid at a neighborhood bar. That kept her in booze, but also kept her out all night and put her in bed or drunk all day. On the rare occasion when he asked for any help, she'd huff and say he was the biggest mistake of her life.

When Buck was ten years old, his mother married an auto mechanic she'd met in the bar. He had promised them a normal life, and for a split second, Buck had hope. But that hope quickly faded when his new stepfather dragged them off to the backwoods of Alabama, took to drinking, and never worked another day in his life. It turned out all he wanted was their guaranteed pension from the military. Once again life took a turn for the worse.

Unable to deal with the mistake she'd made, his mother went back to work as a barmaid. But instead of coming home when her shift was over, she stayed at the bar and drank herself into oblivion. On the rare occasion when she wasn't passed out cold from the night before, she'd yell at him from her bed to get up and go to school. He'd get up, put on the same dirty clothes from the day before, and leave the house, but he rarely made it to school.

The problem was, when Buck finally returned home, his mother was already at work and his stepfather, when he wasn't shitfaced, would force Buck to suck him until his dick was hard and then shove it up Buck's ass. Buck never had a thing he could call his own except his innocence, and that was taken from him too. He was a little boy forced into an adult world with no one to love him or protect him and no power to protect himself. He took the abuse day after day, month after month, year after year. But everything changed the day he turned fifteen.

Buck was ready for his stepfather when he came looking for his usual action. The man didn't see the baseball bat until it hit him in the middle of the forehead. As his stepfather lay on the floor, bleeding and moaning from the pain, Buck said in the most forceful voice he could muster, "If you ever mention my name again or come looking for me, I'll report you for what you've been doing to me for the last five years, and you'll rot in prison. I swear it." He threw the bat on the floor, took the keys to his stepfather's old truck, and walked out.

A year came and went after Buck left Alabama. For the first few months, he'd made his way doing odd jobs and sleeping in his stepfather's truck. He ended up in LaGrange, Georgia, working as a farmhand. He had a roof over his head and food in his mouth, and he was finally starting to build a life for himself. He was free from his bitch of a mother and his stepfather's abuse, and that alone was his motivation. But everything was about to go terribly wrong—again.

One morning he was pulled over by Georgia State Patrol for what he learned was an expired plate. After running the plate, the officer told Buck the truck had been reported stolen and he was under arrest. He was hauled into jail, convicted, and sentenced to five years in prison. Although he kept his promise to expose all the abuse he had suffered, he was told that had no bearing on this case, and he would have to sue his stepfather in a separate action. So in the end, his stepfather won again.

Prison was like going home again. The abuse didn't come directly from his stepfather, but the man was still fucking him over even though Buck was behind a different set of bars. When he was finally released from prison, he came out a different man. He was totally defeated, bitter, and angry at the world. He floated from town to town and finally ended up in Nashville, working for the Lazy H Ranch. He hated shoveling horse shit every day, but one way or the other, he was going to get his due. On an occasional night off, he met Tina. She was older and resembled Tammy Wynette. Although she wasn't that great a singer, he saw her as a way out.

He courted her on his best behavior and convinced her she had a chance at stardom if she allowed him to manage her career. While they were beating the pavement at night, the days were really starting to piss Buck off. The work was hard, the hours were long, and he was tired of it. Just when he was about to go ballistic, the ranch's previous foreman resigned, and he thought he'd be a shoo-in for the job. He interviewed, and the ranch owner said he would consider him, but he would like to look at all his options. Buck bit his lip to keep from going off on the guy and walked out of the office, but underneath he was fuming. He wanted that job, and come hell or high water, he was going to get it.

Buck figured the fewer interviews the owner had, the better chance he had at getting the foreman job, so he sent the first candidate, a guy named Billy Eagan, on a wild goose chase so he'd miss his appointment altogether. But when the owner found him, Buck cursed silently and watched as the two men disappeared inside the massive barn deep in conversation. He was beyond pissed.

As dusk approached, Buck had just stacked the last bale of hay when he saw Eagan and the owner walking toward Eagan's truck. They stopped, turned to each other, spoke another few words, and shook hands, and Buck knew his fate was sealed. His face heated and he swore under his breath, "Damn it. I've damn near killed myself for that asshole, and he owes me this job. I'm going to have the fucking job if it kills me—or someone else. We'll see who the better man is."

BUCK SMILED deviously as the news ended and Jimmy opened his show. When Jimmy announced Billy was up next, Buck was hardly able to control his anticipation. He paced back and forth, unable to wait for the commercial to be over so he could find out how the queer was going to get out of this mess. When the commercial break ended, he sat down, almost salivating from excitement, but when he saw a relaxed Billy and Ian walk onto the set, smiling and waving, he went ballistic.

"What the fuck?" Buck said to himself.

He turned the volume up louder and listened carefully as the interview progressed, and Buck became angrier and angrier with each word. They were making jokes about the queers. Jimmy Fallon was actually defending their sickening love. He listened in complete horror as Billy and Ian told their story and the audience actually applauded them. When the interview was over, Buck threw his beer bottle at the television in a fit of anger. Both the beer bottle and the television exploded from the force, and shards of glass flew everywhere.

"Those motherfucking queers," Buck hissed. "How can that dick lover keep stepping in shit and end up smelling like a rose?"

Buck made a quick decision and dug a ratty old duffel bag out from under the bed. In a fit, he started throwing the few things he owned into it. When it was full, he hurled it at the front door. "Billy Eagan may have nine lives, but let's see how many lives his boyfriend has!"

TWO DAYS later Buck was in Nashville, Tennessee, for the first time in four years. He'd stopped at a truck stop on I-40, hopped on the Internet, and for $12.95 got all the information he needed about Ian Dillon, including his full address. He parked in front of a new construction site about a block down the street from Dillon's house, slouched down low in his truck, and waited. It was Saturday morning, and if anyone questioned him, he could just say he was a construction worker who must have got his schedule wrong. He was going to sit tight and watch Billy and Ian's comings and goings for a couple of days while he developed his plan.

Chapter Six

BILLY AND Ian sat side by side on the couch sipping longnecks, their bare feet up on the ottoman. They, along with Josh, had spent the last few days crisscrossing the country from California to Tennessee, hitting every country radio station in the major markets. They'd be in one state for the morning commute and then another for the afternoon commute. It had been an exhausting schedule, but it had paid off. For the most part, the reception had been very good. A couple of DJs acted cool but had an underlying resentment Billy and Ian both picked up on. Still, those occasions were few and far between. And besides, the stations had complete control of the programming, so even if a DJ had a problem with them personally, they still had to play Billy's songs.

Billy and Ian had arrived home a little after midnight, collapsed from sheer exhaustion, and slept until ten o'clock the next morning. They'd driven out to the ranch, spent the day with Jules and Jean, and after lunch had taken a nice long trail ride. The afternoon had been spent enjoying a leisurely nap in the hammock and had finally ended with one of Jean's home-cooked meals.

"I hate to admit this," Billy said, "because we *are* going to New Orleans to see my family, but the thought of packing again isn't very appealing."

Ian squeezed Billy's leg. "I know. But how about I go and get started, and you can take a couple minutes to call your parents and check in."

"Bless you," Billy said. "What time do we land?"

"I think we told the pilot we were going to leave around nine o'clock, so that should put us there a little after ten," Ian said.

"Then an hour or so to cross the Causeway to the North Shore," Billy added. "So just before lunch, I'd imagine."

"Sounds about right," Ian confirmed, kissing Billy's cheek. "I'll see you upstairs in a little bit."

Billy picked up the phone and dialed his parents' number. As the phone rang, he thought about the peace and quiet of the new home he'd bought his parents two years ago. The house was on the Bogue Falaya River on the North Shore of New Orleans in a little town called Covington. It sat on a couple acres of land that held, in addition to the main house, a guesthouse for him and Ian, and because Billy's father loved to fish, a boat dock. Finally the answering machine picked up, and the cheerful voice of his mother said, "Sorry we missed your call. Please leave us a message, and we'll call you back as soon as we can."

"You're not half as sorry as I am," Billy said. "Just wanted to let you know Ian and I will be arriving tomorrow about lunchtime or a little before. Looking forward to seeing you guys. Call when you get this."

Billy hung up the phone and sighed. "I guess my bags aren't gonna pack themselves."

BUCK HAD finally fallen asleep in his truck after the fags got home sometime around midnight. Seeing the pansies again had had more of an effect on him than he'd expected. He'd woken in a pissed-off mood with a raging hard-on because of the types of dreams he'd had all night long: dreams that involved them. And him. *Fucking queens are messing with my head.*

He drank the last of the lukewarm coffee from his old thermos and peed into a Styrofoam cup. When the garage door finally opened, Buck looked at his watch. *Eleven o'clock.* He waited for them to pass him by and then turned his truck around and tailed them from a reasonable distance, following them onto I-40, careful to stay several cars back. When he saw the exit they were taking, he knew exactly where they were headed.

As they turned in under the etched iron sign of the Lazy H Ranch, Buck kept going straight, turned around about a half mile down the road, and ducked onto a dirt road with a view of the ranch entrance.

By the time they exited the ranch almost seven hours later, he'd filled up four more Styrofoam cups of pee and was hungry enough to eat his own arm.

Buck kept them in sight all the way back to Westhaven, right up until they pulled into their driveway and disappeared behind the closing garage door. He took this opportunity to get a bite to eat and go to the bathroom and was back in his spot within an hour.

The next morning around seven thirty, the garage door opened again, and Buck eased up in his seat a little. Eagan was loading luggage into the back of car. "No!" Buck hissed. "Motherfucker! Where are they going now?"

Then Buck relaxed a little when he remembered Eagan had mentioned to Jimmy Fallon they were taking a trip to New Orleans to visit his family. *That might work out even better. New Orleans, here I come.*

Buck followed them to the airport to make sure they were actually leaving, but he couldn't really be sure if they were going to New Orleans or not. He'd have to take a chance on that one. He then drove to another truck stop, searched the Internet for information on Billy's parents, and after another $12.95, had their name and address. He printed off directions to New Orleans, filled his truck with gas, and hit the highway. He wasn't really sure what he was going to do when he got there, but he felt certain an opportunity would present itself to allow him to finish his plan.

IAN AND Billy touched down at Louis Armstrong New Orleans International Airport, picked up a rental car, and headed east on I-10 to Metairie, where they drove onto the twenty-six-mile bridge known as the Causeway to cross Lake Pontchartrain to the North Shore of New Orleans.

As planned they pulled into Billy's parents' driveway before lunch, and when Billy opened the car door, he was assaulted with fresh air and the slightest hint of something cooking. *Smells like home!*

Before Ian could get out of the car, the atrium door of the house flew open and Billy's mother was jumping into his arms. Ian watched as she held him protectively, coddling her only son.

Ian got out of the rented SUV, stood on the running board, rested his elbows on the roof, and peered at the duo. "Man, I wish I'd had a mother like you," he said to Vicki.

"Oh, Ian. You're so sweet," Vicki said. "But remember you have Jean and now me, so we're the next best thing. Now get over here and give your mom a hug."

Ian hopped down and took Vicki into his arms.

When he released her, Vicki stepped back and looked at the two of them. "Aren't you two a sight for sore eyes? You both look great," she added. "A little tired, but great."

"Last week was a really long week," Billy explained.

"I'll bet it was," Vicki said. "I watched you boys on every television show that aired here, and y'all looked mighty handsome."

"Thanks, ma'am," Ian said.

"Yeah, Mama," Billy said, looking around. "Thanks. Where's Daddy?"

"Oh, he's fiddling around down at the boat dock. I swear, since you put that thing in, he's never in the house anymore."

"Mind if we take a walk down and find him?" Billy asked.

"Not at all," Vicki said. "I've got my world-famous gumbo simmering on the stove, and all I've got to do is toss the salad. You boys don't waste too much time down there. We'll eat in about thirty minutes."

"Yes, ma'am," Billy said.

"And by the way, your sisters and their families are joining us for dinner tonight," Vicki said. "I hope that's okay?"

"Of course it is," Ian said before Billy could respond. "It'll be fun."

Vicki disappeared through the door she'd popped out of, and Billy and Ian walked around the house to the pool area and then on to the stone path leading to the river. Billy could see his dad hosing off his boat, which was in a lift alongside the dock. When his dad

75

saw them, he waved and both Billy and Ian waved back. He put down the hose and started walking in their direction.

When they met, John took his son into his arms. "Good to see you, boy."

"Good to see you too, Daddy."

"Ian," John said. "Don't be shy. Give the old man a hug."

It warmed Billy's heart to see them take to Ian so well. They knew Ian made their only son happy, and that was all it took. They loved Ian now as much as they loved him, and they'd made him an official member of the family.

Of course, in the beginning Billy's father hadn't always been this supportive. Early on they hadn't had long conversations or discussions about Billy's sexuality. When Billy originally told his dad he was gay, the man had simply nodded, told him he loved him, and left the room. Billy had always wondered if his dad had been hurt, disappointed, or just ashamed to have a gay son, but he'd been too afraid to ask. He didn't think it made a difference, because either of the options would hurt equally, so he'd just let it go. Luckily over the years, John had come around nicely and even said on more than one occasion how grateful he was for the man Billy had become.

Deep down Billy had always had his own guilt issues about being gay, because he was the only Eagan boy left in the family line, and if he didn't produce a son, the family name would die when he did. His father had mentioned it several times before he knew Billy was gay, but once Billy had come out to him, he'd never brought it up again, and that had hurt Billy deeply. Billy remembered wanting to scream that he didn't have to be straight to produce a child, but as always he'd kept his mouth shut and buried his feelings when it came to his father.

Soon after falling in love with Ian and realizing he finally had someone to share his life with, he'd also realized that the possibility existed they could have children together one day. The guilt he'd felt previously had lessened immensely. He and Ian hadn't discussed having children of their own at any length yet, but he felt better simply knowing it was an option.

Billy was shaken out of his thoughts by his dad's voice. "You boys are both looking well," John said. "And so busy. Your mama and me stayed up way past our bedtime to watch you boys on television. You did a great job. I'm proud of you both."

Billy simply nodded, fighting the lump in his throat he always got when his father said he was proud of him.

"Thanks, John," Ian said, watching Billy struggle. "What's going on down here?"

"Went fishing this morning and was just rinsing off the boat."

"Catch anything?" Billy asked.

"Nothing but a sunburn," John teased. "We better get up to the house, though. Your mama's gonna have lunch ready soon."

"You two go on ahead," Billy said. "I'm gonna walk on down to the river, sit on the dock for a few minutes and catch my breath."

"You okay?" Ian asked.

"I'm real good," Billy replied. "I just want to take a few minutes to listen to the quiet."

Billy realized Ian would have preferred to walk down to the river with him, but Ian, knowing John well by now, probably figured he would want to tag along also, so Ian did what he always did and sheltered Billy, making sure he was able to escape when he needed to.

Billy kissed Ian on the cheek, and then he turned and headed for the river. He heard Ian and John laughing and talking as they made their way back up the stone path to the house, and that made him smile.

It had been five years since Ian had come into his life, and although it had been a rocky first year, things had settled down and now they were rock solid. He felt so much lighter now that his and Ian's relationship was out there and they no longer had to hide.

Billy stepped up onto the dock, took a deep breath, inhaling the fresh county air, and looked out over the river. There wasn't a sound except an occasional seagull and the water making its way down the river to the lake. Billy took a moment to thank God for all he'd been blessed with and then turned around and saw Ian and his parents standing on the patio watching him. He waved, and they waved back before disappearing into the house.

Billy took a seat on one of the chaise lounges at the end of the dock and rested his head in his hands. He realized suddenly that having so much love in his life meant he had that much more to lose. He didn't know why, but something was bothering him. He couldn't put his finger on it, but it was nagging at the back of his mind. This outing, as they called it, had gone so easily. He, Ian, and Josh had all been prepared for a legal battle with Capitol and the real threat of Billy losing his career. But nothing had come of it. With a little encouragement, Mike had supported them, and the same was true of what they'd seen of the general public. Could it all be behind them that easily? He hoped so, but he couldn't shake the feeling that it wasn't over just yet.

Billy felt a hand on his shoulder, and he instinctively recognized Ian's touch. He cocked one eye open and looked up into Ian's green eyes.

"You okay, Cowboy?"

Billy laid his hand over Ian's. "Absolutely," he proclaimed. "I just needed to settle my brain a little. It's been a crazy week."

"Any regrets?" Ian asked.

"Not a one," Billy said, pulling Ian down to sit between his open legs. "I'm the luckiest man alive."

"Then what's bothering you?" Ian asked softly.

Billy smiled. "Sometimes I hate that you know me so well."

"So?"

"I don't know," Billy said honestly. "I can't seem to put my finger on it, but I feel like all the potential drama went way too well. And I guess I'm nervous waiting for the other shoe to drop."

"Well, then," Ian said, "if and when that happens, we'll deal with it together like we always do."

"Deal," Billy said, kissing Ian gently.

"Your mother sent me out here to get you," Ian warned. "So we better start heading back."

"I know. If her gumbo gets cold, I'm in for it. Country superstar or not."

Ian stood and pulled Billy to his feet. "I love you, Cowboy."

"I love you too."

BUCK'S ROUTE took him down I-65 south to Birmingham, Alabama. He caught I-59 down to Meridian, Mississippi, and then Hattiesburg and eventually into New Orleans. Buck was five hours into his trip and approaching Meridian when he stopped for gas. While he pumped, his mind was still on overload. In the time since he'd left Nashville, he'd figured out exactly what he wanted to do, but until he got to New Orleans, he couldn't figure out how he was going to do it. Getting these two queers apart was definitely going to be the tough part. But hopefully with some diligence and a little luck, a situation might present itself that Buck would be able to take advantage of. He would have to wait and see, and for him, that was the toughest part.

Since he'd left Nashville, he had been plagued by flashbacks of the dreams he'd had of Billy, Ian, and, well… him. The vivid Technicolor memories popped in and out of his mind so many times he finally turned up the radio as loud as it would go and sang every song he knew to combat the mental intrusions. But eventually even that stopped working, and when the next memory produced a full-on erection, he did what he used to do to kill his hard-on when his stepfather was raping him: he punched his fist into his crotch over and over with such force it brought tears to his eyes, and he cried out in agony.

That stopped the memories—for a while anyway. The more he drove, the angrier he got. He kept telling himself that what he was going to do to them was never for his pleasure, but only for their pain. But somewhere deep down he knew the real truth.

I should have killed that motherfucking rapist when I had the chance instead of just knocking him out.

BILLY AND Ian crawled into bed a little before eleven thirty that night. "Man! Am I beat," Billy said as he rolled over onto his stomach and rested his head on his folded arms.

Ian chuckled. "That sure looks like a plea for a back rub to me."

"Whatever do you mean," Billy teased. "But if you insist, I wouldn't deprive you of that pleasure."

"Oh, I get it. You're only doing this for me," Ian said as he crawled onto Billy's back and straddled his ass.

"Of course. Everything I do is for you."

Ian kneaded Billy's shoulders and realized he was extremely tense, even for Billy, who was keyed up most of the time. "You need to relax, Cowboy," Ian whispered. "You're as tense as a tightrope."

"I'm trying, but I just can't shake this feeling that something wicked this way comes."

Ian squeezed and rubbed Billy's neck. "I can't imagine what that would be, but if something does come up, we'll handle it like we deal with everything else."

Billy rolled over underneath Ian and looked into his eyes. "How did I get so lucky?"

"We're both lucky," Ian said as he leaned down and kissed Billy gently. "It was a fun night."

"It was fun," Billy agreed. "But the questions were like rapid fire. 'Was Ellen DeGeneres nice? What was Jimmy Fallon really like? Is Letterman's humor as dry as it seems like on television? Is Conan really that tall? Did Robin Roberts ask for your autograph? Is Carson as cute in person as he is on The Voice?' By the end of the night, I was sick of telling everyone step by step what it was like to be on a talk show."

"That *was* really funny, but you handled it so well," Ian said. "Give them a break. That's exciting stuff."

"Thanks, and you're right. I forget how exciting this all is to them. Hell! I love 'em all to death, and I'd answer every single one again if they asked."

"I know. And they seemed really pleased that we are going to buy a house here," Ian said.

"Seriously," Billy admitted. "I'm really excited to start looking myself."

"How much of a coincidence was it that your sister Lynn's friend had recently sold Sandra Bullock her house in the Garden District? Once she made that call, we were in like Flint."

"It couldn't have worked out any better." Billy said.

Ian felt something poking him in the ass, so he slid off of Billy, settled at his side, and grabbed Billy's erection through his underwear. "It looks like something else is begging for a little attention as well."

BUCK MADE it to New Orleans, found Billy's parents' house, and parked on the opposite side of the street in front of a wooded area about a block down. The lots were so big in this neighborhood there were expanses of wooded areas on both sides of all the houses. He was lucky he'd found a spot with a great view of the front porch and driveway. He'd been here for six and a half hours, and although he'd seen a number of people coming and going, there was no sign of Eagan or Dillon. He'd loaded up on coffee and cheeseburgers from McDonald's on the way, so he was settled in for the night.

Tomorrow will present more options. I just know it.

Chapter Seven

VICKI FIXED a huge breakfast, and Ian and Billy ate like it was going out of style. Being on the road for a week and eating nothing but hotel, restaurant, or fast food had killed them both, but they were so making up for it now.

They had to hurry because they were meeting the Realtor at her Magazine Street office at ten o'clock. From there they were going to preview ten houses in the French Quarter, the Irish Channel, and the Garden District. The one Billy had been the most excited about was in the 3700 block of St. Charles Avenue and had been previously owned by Anne Rice as her personal home. The grand old house was rumored to be the inspiration for the Mayfair Witch house referred to in many of her vampire novels. The pictures they'd looked at online last night were stunning. The house was quite grand, and even included a ballroom.

Ian had been equally impressed but thought it might be too much house for them. He agreed to keep an open mind, and he liked the fact that it was on a Mardi Gras parade route. And they were both tickled because it came with a 1969 stretch limousine. "How fun would that be?" Billy had asked.

They backed out of the driveway at eight forty-five sharp, crossed the Causeway again, caught I-10 east to downtown, and exited at Magazine Street near the Mississippi River. Billy followed the directions and parked two blocks away in a lot that belonged to the New Orleans Property Shop real estate office. Then he and Ian strolled leisurely down Magazine Street to the provided address.

A few people recognized Billy, and as usual, he stopped and signed a couple of autographs and took a few selfies before they continued on. He had the feeling they were being watched, but he got that all of the time when he was in public. As they walked along, he noticed Magazine Street was lined with antique stores, restaurants, and specialty shops on both sides of the street, but one building caught Billy's attention. It was right next to the real estate office, and the sign painted on the window said Bissonet & Cruz, Private Investigators. The building had an old-timey appearance, like something you would see in a nostalgic black-and-white film, and he expected Humphrey Bogart to step out of the front door at any time. He stopped and simply stared up at the edifice in wonder. "This is such a cool building," he mumbled.

"It is," Ian agreed. "But we need to go inside. We're a couple minutes late." Ian took his hand and dragged him into the office right next door. Their Realtor was named Stella Worley, and she was at the front desk ready to greet them.

"It's really nice to meet you," she said, looking between Ian and Billy. "Lynn has talked about you both nonstop."

"Nice to meet you as well," Billy said.

Some of the female agents, as well as one of the male agents, came up and introduced themselves and asked if they could take a couple of selfies, and of course Billy was happy to do it.

BUCK PARKED a block down, got out, and shoved a few quarters in the meter. He didn't know how long he was going to be here, but he certainly didn't want to blow his cover over a parking ticket. He watched Eagan and Dillon turn into a parking lot and then start to walk in his direction. He was on the verge of panicking, but then he remembered he looked very different now, and these guys weren't expecting to see him here. He slid down as far as he could without being too obvious. Luckily the men walked right past him without a second glance.

Buck followed them in his rearview and passenger side mirrors and tracked them as they walked into a real estate office. *Buying some property, are we?*

Not more than fifteen minutes later, Dillon and Eagan exited the real estate office with a nicely dressed woman, and the three of them started walking back in his direction. He slouched down again when they passed by his truck, and then he followed their movements as they got into a black Mercedes parked in the same parking lot. When they exited the lot, Buck started his truck and pulled out behind them. He followed them as they turned right on Third Street, proceeded a few more blocks, and stopped in front of a house on the corner of Third and Coliseum. He stayed back a block or so and continued to spy on them as they walked around the exterior of the house and then disappeared through the front door.

"THIS IS fantastic," Ian said, gazing up at the twelve-foot-plus ceiling in the foyer.

"Beautiful, isn't it?" Stella said. "Every room in the house has fourteen-foot ceilings."

They continued down the long hall and saw the formal living room to the right and the formal dining room to the left. Billy's eyes were darting from here to there, taking in every detail. The massive rooms had extrawide dentil crown molding, highly polished hardwood floors, and custom draperies throughout. The decor was very tasteful as well. "The rooms are so voluminous," Billy commented, looking around.

They continued back to a gourmet kitchen, den, and sunroom. Upstairs were four bedrooms, all with en suite bathrooms, and an office fit for the president of the United States.

"This is just lovely," Ian said. "I think it's a little formal for us, but it's really lovely."

"I think you're right," Billy agreed. "But I like the square footage."

"Yeah, the size is really good, but it's also not on the parade route."

"That's true," Stella said. "Albeit only a few blocks from St. Charles. But let's mark this one off the list."

"I'm glad we saw it, though," Ian added. "It's quite a showplace."

"That's the fun of house hunting," Stella agreed with a laugh.

Their next stop was at the house Billy was salivating to see. They pulled up in front of 3711 St. Charles Avenue, and the structure was even more impressive than the pictures. The beveled cut-glass front door was massive and was framed perfectly by the porch stretching across the front and down the left side of the house.

When they walked through the front door, they were again amazed at the ceiling height and the massive rooms. Billy glanced at the formal living room to the right, but was immediately drawn across the hall to the huge ballroom.

This is exactly what I would expect Anne Rice's former house to look like.

A gigantic window graced the wall directly across from the large pocket doors leading into the room. Under the window was an enormous banquette, flanked by a fireplace on each end. The crystal chandelier was huge and had matching wall sconces every four feet or so all the way around the room. But the most impressive feature was that everything from the crown molding to the baseboards and window trim was done in gilt.

Just like the house in the Mayfair Witch novels I read a long time ago.

To the right, more colossal pocket doors opened into an adjoining dining room, which led on to the caterer's kitchen and maid's quarters.

They continued up the grand staircase and toured the rest of the house, each room more impressive than the last.

"This is some house," Billy said.

"That's an understatement," Ian agreed. "How much are they asking for this?"

Stella looked at her listings sheet. "Just under $2.2 million," she said.

"Worth every penny," Ian admitted.

Back downstairs they walked out onto the side porch and under the breezeway that connected the garage to the main house.

"And the pièce de résistance," Stella said as she opened the garage door.

There it was: the 1969 shiny black stretch limousine. Billy ran his hand along the side and searched his memory, trying to remember if it had appeared in any of Anne's novels. But for the life of him, he couldn't remember. He made a mental note to look that up when he got to a computer.

Ian took out his phone and took a picture of Billy in front of the limo. "Billy! I can see you riding around New Orleans in this thing. What fun!"

"Hardly," Billy teased. "A pickup truck is more my speed." Then he grabbed Ian's hand. "Ian, I want this house. Please. Please. Please."

"Seriously?" Ian said. "It's huge. What would we do with all the space?"

"Who cares," Billy replied, "I love it."

"It's just as formal as the last one," Ian reminded him. "And that ballroom? It's even more formal."

"But can you imagine the parties at New Year's Eve, Halloween, and Mardi Gras? We can make everyone dress up in period clothing. Or better yet. Vampire attire. That would be so cool." A smile spread across Billy's face.

"I can see you're really getting into this Anne Rice thing," Ian said.

"Is it that obvious? I mean… I read all her books growing up, and I loved them."

"Look," Ian proclaimed, "you're not going to make me be the practical one here and ruin your fantasy. If you want it, I'm all for it. But…," he continued. "Let's just look at a few more to make sure we've seen everything there is to see."

"That makes sense," Billy said. "But Ian… I. Have. To. Have. This. House."

"Oh jeez," Ian said to Stella. "So dramatic, this one is."

Stella laughed and suggested they move to the next house on the list. It was in the French Quarter in the one thousand block of Royal Street between St. Philip and Ursuline streets. They drove down St. Charles Avenue, around Lee Circle, crossed Canal Street, and were in the French Quarter. Stella drove by the front of the house, pulled to the side of Royal Street, and stopped.

"Here it is," she said. "Now I know it doesn't look like much from the street, but wait until you see the potential inside."

Billy studied the structure. It was a typical French Quarter dwelling. It was about twenty feet wide and bumped up against another house to the left, with a small alley on the right and another house next to the narrow alley. It was three stories tall, with wrought iron railings across the second and third floor balconies.

"Now this is pure speculation on my part," Stella said, "because we've never talked about renovating, but I thought I'd show it to you anyway. It's completely gutted inside except for the free-standing staircase that leads to the second and third floors."

Stella put her blinker on and pulled out onto Royal Street again. "Parking is around the corner." She continued to explain her thought process. "This is a clean slate, or a blank canvas if you prefer. You can totally make this your own by going as formal or as casual as you like."

She turned left at the next block and turned left again, stopping at a wrought iron gate. She looked at her notes. "Four, two, four, two," she said out loud as she pressed the four-digit code into the keypad. "You have your own private alley and parking space for two cars, which is almost unheard of in the French Quarter. Most people have to buy or rent parking spaces in the few garages in the area. At a very hefty price, I might add."

The gate opened, and Stella drove down an alley that ended in two parking spaces as she'd described. They got out of the car and walked through another wrought iron gate, and a beautiful bricked courtyard unfolded in front of them. A plunging pool in the center was surrounded by chaise lounges, and the walls on either side were at least twenty feet high. They were covered almost completely in espaliered ivy, and it was extremely private. A lion's head plastered to the wall spit water into a small pond below.

"Let me warn you, this is where the beauty stops, fellas," Stella said. "For now. But I guarantee this place will not be on the market long and will be stunning when it's complete."

"Who cares if the inside is ever finished," Ian said. "I'll just live out here."

"Me too," Billy agreed.

Stella turned the doorknob and pushed open the unlocked door. "So let's go take a look."

"It's unlocked?" Ian asked.

"Yeah. There's nothing really to steal," Stella said. "The workers are here most days, and if you take into consideration the security gate, there's really no need to lock it."

"Good point," Ian said.

As they entered the first floor from the courtyard, they saw the curved backside of a freestanding stairway midway through the expanse and a vast open space stripped down to the bare floor.

"You weren't kidding when you said it was gutted," Billy said.

"There's about fifteen hundred square feet on each of the first two floors and just over a thousand on the third, totaling over four thousand square feet," Stella explained.

"Plenty enough space," Billy said.

"And I like the fact that we can make this our own, Billy," Ian said.

"I like that too."

Ian looked around. "I mean… it's not on the parade route, but I guess I can trade that for the French Quarter."

"I agree," Billy said.

"Let's go upstairs," Stella suggested.

The three of them walked to the front of the empty space and turned around. The freestanding staircase started against the wall on the left side of the room and curved all the way up to the right side of the second floor. "Wow," Ian said. "This stairway is really impressive."

"I'll say," Billy agreed, looking up at the structure. "I still love the allure of the Rice house, but I'm starting to see the potential in this space as well."

Stella piped in again. "Well if you like this staircase, there's another one just like it from the second floor to the third."

Billy looked at Ian, whose smile was beaming. *I think he likes this one.*

They started up the stairs and saw the same exact footprint as down below except for the fact that it had a balcony in the front overlooking Royal Street and another one in back overlooking the courtyard.

Stella walked to the front of the room, opened one of the four french doors, and motioned for Ian and Billy to join her. "The gallery," she said.

"Gallery?" Billy asked.

"That's what they are called in the French Quarter if they are held up with posts," Stella explained.

"I grew up here, and I never knew that," Billy shared.

He and Ian followed Stella and stood at the railing looking down at Royal Street. "Now Matthew McConaughey lives right across the street," she pointed out.

"How convenient," Billy said, dodging a smack from Ian.

They walked into the main space again, crossed and went through the rear french doors onto the second balcony, which overlooked the rear courtyard.

"The courtyard is even more impressive from up here," Billy said.

"We still have one more floor to go, guys," Stella said, leading them back in and up the second set of freestanding stairs.

When they reached the third floor, Billy immediately pictured the master suite. He walked it off, and at about fifty feet by twenty feet, it could easily accommodate their master bedroom and bath, a workout room, and an office for Ian. *This floor could be the perfect place to escape to, all our own.*

Billy watched Ian mulling about, and he could see Ian's wheels were already turning. He knew how Ian's mind worked, and right now he was erecting walls, positioning furniture, and deciding where his soaking tub was going to go. And that was enough for Billy.

"I don't think we need to see any more," Billy said.

Ian turned and flashed such an expression of disappointment, it broke Billy's heart. "We'll take it," he said.

The sadness immediately turned to a big smile full of wonder and excitement. "Seriously?" Ian asked. "We don't even know the price. And what about Anne Rice's house and that limo?"

"Who cares what the price is? And that house is way too gaudy for us anyway," Billy huffed. "And if we want a limo, we'll buy one of our own."

Ian ran across the room and jumped into Billy's arms. "This is going to be so cool. Are you sure?"

"I'm sure," Billy agreed. "I think this is the perfect place for us."

Stella took them back to her office, wrote up an offer, and Billy and Ian signed it.

"The seller has twenty-four hours to respond, so we'll keep our fingers crossed. But…," Stella added, "I think this is a more-than-fair offer."

BUCK PARKED on Magazine Street again, this time across the street a little over a block down, but still with a clear view of the real estate office. He'd followed these idiots all over the city. But he was full of hope. When he'd seen the Mercedes pull over and stop with Eagan hanging out of the window, he'd known what house they were looking at. When they continued on, so did he, but he slowed when he passed the house and looked in through the large windows. He saw all the way through from the front window to the back of the house without interruption, so he figured the house must either be under construction or recently gutted.

This might just be the break I've been waiting for.

When Eagan and Dillon got back into their SUV and headed back to I-10 West, Buck returned to Royal Street. He parked his car, walked to the house, and peered in through the window. *Yes! I was right. It is gutted.*

Buck walked around the corner and nonchalantly strolled back and forth in front of the gate, checking the place out. He heard a vehicle coming up the street and ducked to the side when a truck pulled up to the security gate and stopped. He fumbled in his pocket for a cigarette, bowed his head as he put the cigarette in his mouth, and lit it. The truck had a sign on the door that said French Quarter Restoration. Buck watched from the corner of his eye as the driver punched four, two, four, two into the keypad, ignoring the presence of a man pausing for a cigarette, and the gate began to open slowly. *Bingo!* "Four, two, four, two," he whispered to himself. *This is my lucky day. Now all they need to do is buy this place and everything will fall into place.*

Buck got in his truck and headed back to the North Shore. He remembered passing a library on St. Charles Avenue earlier that day when he was tailing the black Mercedes; that was the easiest place to get free access to a computer and the Internet. He checked in at the front desk, told the librarian he'd just moved to the area and his cable and Internet hadn't been installed yet, and wondered if he could use their computer to check his e-mail. The librarian handed him an application for a temporary library card, and he completed it using a bogus name and an address on Third Street. He almost panicked and darted when she told him to step in front of a camera so she could take his picture for his permanent library card, but he told himself to stay calm. He looked nothing like he had back then.

Buck stepped in front of the little screen, and the librarian moved the countertop camera back and forth until she was satisfied. "Say cheese," she said seconds before the flash went off. She studied the computer screen, then turned the screen around and showed Buck his mug shot.

"Very nice, don't you think?" she asked.

He nodded and smiled.

"Perfect. I'll show you where the computer area is, and you can get started."

Buck chose the computer farthest away from prying eyes and sat down. The first thing he searched for was an over-the-counter concoction that, if injected, would instantly knock someone out. After scanning page after page, he realized there was no homemade remedy that would knock someone out cold in seconds or even minutes. The only possibility that might actually work was a highly concentrated dose of some type of drug like Valium or Xanax dissolved in water. *I'm in New Orleans; I should be able to score some Valium or Xanax somewhere in the French Quarter.*

Just in case, he searched again using the same criteria but this time for something inhaled instead of injected. Again, more garbage popped up, but no real solutions. Finally, as he was about to give up, a site suggested chloroform or ether. Either, if inhaled, could knock someone out instantly. But as he read further, he determined that neither lasted long if not continuously inhaled. In addition, chloroform could be fatal if not done properly. He didn't want to kill Dillon right away. He had plans, after all, and he certainly wanted to save the end for when Eagan would be able to watch.

Fuck! Neither one of those options will work either. I've got to get my hands on some Valium. Enough! Deal with that part later, Buck.

Buck attempted to clear the history on the computer, but that option was not available, apparently turned off, probably for this very reason. But he figured if and when anyone linked any of this back to him, he'd be long gone.

His next search was for the most devastated areas of New Orleans in the aftermath of Hurricane Katrina. He got an overview by parish and scanned article after article. The 9th Ward and the Chalmette areas were badly hit, the most remote, and the slowest to recover. Then he tried to get an idea where those areas were in comparison to the French Quarter, and bingo! Both were within a thirty-minute drive.

While he had time, he made plans to check out both areas to see if he could find a deserted and remote location where he could take Dillon and hold him until he could lure Eagan to join them. He printed off general directions to both areas and fled the library, politely thanking the librarian on the way out.

Buck drove to the Chalmette area first, as it was the farthest away, and was amazed at what he saw. When he was scanning the articles about the hurricane and the cleanup efforts, he'd read that so many homes were underwater and so many lives were lost, the authorities had spray painted the number of dead bodies pulled from each home to keep count block by block. And there it was right in front of him. Many areas and neighborhoods were still deserted. Some boarded-up houses still bore the spray-painted numbers, and the impression it left was eerie—even to Buck, who wasn't the least bit squeamish.

He came across a few stretches of deserted houses, but by and large, every other house was already renovated, and others were under construction. *This won't work! I hope the 9th Ward is in worse shape.*

He followed his directions to the 9th Ward and found stretches and stretches of boarded-up homes with no signs of life. Buck thought the scene looked like a ghost town in one of those old western movies he'd watched as a kid. He smiled to himself. *Now things are looking up.*

Buck parked in front of one particular house that had a two-car garage—which might come in handy to conceal his truck—got out, and walked around the structure. The back door to the house was unlocked, so he let himself in. The house had been gutted down to the studs and would probably work out fine for his needs. But on the way back to his truck again, off in the distance he saw a group of deserted buildings that resembled a school campus or small hospital or something similar. He drove to the location and saw a marquee that read Alfred Lawless High School. At closer inspection it appeared the campus had once held six buildings. There were three buildings still standing and what looked to be three former foundations with nothing standing atop the footings. One of the remaining buildings looked to have been moved completely off of its foundation but was still standing.

He parked, opened the unlocked gate, and drove around the back of the first building. To his amazement, he found three large metal doors that appeared to be some sort of a loading area, with a crooked sign that said Food Deliveries, Bin 2. The building must have housed the school cafeteria.

Buck tried to open the first door, but it was jammed shut. On closer inspection he saw the door was completely off the track. He tried the next one, and luckily it opened with little effort. He drove his truck inside and closed the large door behind him. After finding

93

an unlocked door that led from the storage area into the building proper, Buck went in search of a remote location deep inside that might better suit his needs. He didn't have to look far; he discovered what was left of an abandoned cafeteria, and much to his delight, it had a large walk-in refrigerator. The structure was freestanding in the back corner of the kitchen and measured about fifteen feet by fifteen feet. He opened the door and was immediately assaulted by a musty smell of mold and mildew. He turned his head, took a breath of fresh air, and then looked inside. The interior was empty except for a shelving unit on the far wall and seemed to be the perfect place to hold his hostage. He closed the door again and heard the latch catch. *Great! It still locks!*

He continued snooping, found a couple of cafeteria tables and an old metal school desk nearby, and dragged them into the refrigerator.

This will work out just fine!

IAN WOKE to the sound of his cell phone ringing. He looked at the clock. *Seven fifty-five.*

Billy had gotten up at five o'clock to go fishing with his dad, and Ian had fallen back into a deep sleep.

Ian reached for his phone and looked at the caller ID.

"Stella?" Ian whispered, sitting up. "Good morning, Stella," he answered out loud.

"Hi, Ian," the Realtor said in a cheerful voice. "I hope it's not too early. Did I wake you?"

"It isn't too early, and you did wake me, to answer your question," Ian said teasingly. "But it's time to get up anyway. Do you have good news for us?"

"I do," she said. "The seller accepted your offer."

"Yessss," Ian said.

"But…," Stella added.

"Uh-oh!" Ian murmured into the phone.

"They want to close in a week. Now, before you panic, I talked to my legal department, and they can do everything that needs to be done on our end if we get clear title, and of course that's the seller's responsibility and... if you guys can provide the funds."

"The funds won't be a problem," Ian replied. "Billy's out fishing with his dad, but I'll give him a call and get right back to you."

"I'll be here," she said cheerily. "Oh, and one more thing, Ian. I talked to the inspector a little while ago, and because of the short turnaround time before closing, he wants to inspect the property this morning at eleven o'clock. I have a closing this morning, so I'm going to postpone another inspection my assistant was handling and send her over to your place."

"No," Ian said. "Don't do that. I'll meet the inspector over there. Billy and I were hoping to go back over and look at the property again anyway. I'll go over this morning alone."

"Are you sure?" Stella asked. "I hate to put you out."

"You're not putting me out. And besides, I'd like to be there while he does his inspection anyway."

"Perfect," Stella said. "Just call me back after you talk to Billy."

"Will do."

Ian ended the call and dialed Billy's cell phone.

He answered on the second ring. "Morning, sunshine."

"Hey, Cowboy. I've got good news."

"About the house?"

"Yep. They accepted our offer, but... they want to close in seven days."

"I don't see a problem with that," Billy said. "The money is there."

"How are we gonna do this?" Ian asked.

"I've got more than enough money to pay for this," Billy said.

"So do I," Ian responded, "but I want this to be our house together."

"Then let's go fifty-fifty for now."

"What do you mean *for now*?" Ian asked.

"Since we've gone public with our relationship, I don't see any reason why we shouldn't go ahead and pool our finances," Billy said. "Unless you want to keep them separate?"

"Of course not," Ian said. "But you know you have way more money than I have."

"Money I may have made on paper, but money we both earned," Billy corrected.

"If you say so," Ian said. "I'll call our accountant later and instruct him to wire half the money into my checking account immediately and then have him start the process of combining our funds."

"And I'll do the same," Billy said. "It should be a fairly painless process."

"Oh," Ian said. "I almost forgot. Stella has a closing this morning, and I agreed to meet the inspector at eleven, so I won't be here when you get back."

"Do you want me come back now and go with you?"

"Don't be silly," Ian protested. "Since the house is down to its studs, it will only be an inspection of the structure, so it shouldn't take more than an hour or so."

"Are you sure?"

"Absolutely. Enjoy yourself, and I'll see you when I get back."

"Okay. If you insist," Billy said hesitantly. "Love you."

"I love you too. Have fun."

Ian glanced at the clock again. *Eight thirty. I might as well shower, grab a quick bite, and head over there. I'd like to look around again before we get an architect to start working on the plans.*

BACK ON the North Shore, Buck sat in his truck in his usual perch, watching for any activity. He was extremely exhausted and fought to keep his eyes open. After he'd set up his "torture chamber," as he called it, he'd left the Alfred Lawless High School and driven to the first Walmart he'd found. With the help of a high-school-aged sales clerk, he found the syringes and some other supplies and then headed straight back to the French Quarter. He needed drugs, and the only way he saw to get them was to stalk every back alley until he found what he was looking for. And he did just that. By three o'clock the next morning, he had twelve Valium and twelve Xanax. It had cost him two hundred bucks, but it was going to be well worth the price.

He'd spent the better part of two hours crushing the pills and dissolving them in water. He'd stirred constantly until the mixture became a pure creamy liquid, then separated the mixture into thirds and loaded them into three syringes.

He sat up when he saw the SUV back out of the driveway. *What? Can I really be this lucky?*

Dillon was alone. But where was he going?

Buck started his engine, put the truck in drive, and followed Ian through downtown Covington, over the Causeway and back to I-10 West. But this time Ian took the Slidell exit and used the Vieux Carré off-ramp. He turned right on Esplanade Avenue to Royal Street and turned right again. *He's going back to that house! Is this my lucky day or what?*

Buck was giddy with excitement. He patted the top pocket of his shirt, fingered the three syringes, and smiled. He watched Dillon pull up to the wrought iron gate and punch in the security code. He circled the block a few times and then approached the gate himself. He held his breath as he punched in four, two, four, two. When the gate began to open, he released his breath. *So far, so good.*

Buck pulled into the spot next to the SUV, removed one of the syringes from his top pocket, and held it in his hand. He exited his truck and walked through another gate that led to a patio of some sort. Buck saw the back door to the dwelling was open and headed that way. He froze when he heard a cell phone ringing. In a state of panic, he reached for his, but before he could check, the ringing stopped. He heard Dillon's voice.

"Hey, Todd. How's it going?"

Buck stepped back against the wall and stayed out of sight.

"Great to hear it. Yeah, I guess you saw, huh?

"Wasn't that a piece of shit? I mean… come on, the *National Intruder*? But Billy always says everything happens for a reason. And in the end, the story turned out to be a blessing in disguise."

Blessing, my ass!

"We have no idea who the source was, but I wish I did so I could thank them personally."

Your wish is about to come true, asshole!

"No worries. We knew it wasn't you or Luke. Hey, on the lighter side of the news, Billy and I just bought a house in the French Quarter."

So they did buy this place.

"Yeah, in New Orleans. It's gutted, so we're totally going to be able to make it our own. I think it's gonna be great.

"Billy? He's fishing with his dad, and I'm here at the new house meeting the inspector—" Buck saw Dillon look down at his watch. "—who's due here in about thirty minutes."

Fuck! I sure hope the guy's not early.

"Let me call you back, Todd. I want to take another look around before the inspector gets here."

It's show time!

Dillon looked around the open area and started up the stairs before Buck could approach him.

Even better! Less chance of being seen upstairs.

Buck waited until he heard footsteps overhead to follow Dillon up the stairs. When he reached the top of the stairs, he saw Dillon standing at the other end of the room gazing out of the doors looking over the street. He had rested one hand on the doorsill and still held his cell phone in his other hand. Buck approached as slowly and quietly as possible, and when he was right up on Dillon and about to strike, Dillon turned and gasped.

"Oh God. You scared me," Dillon said, beginning to laugh.

"Sorry, sir," Buck said keeping his head as far down as he could without being too obvious.

Dillon looked at him curiously. "You must be the inspector," he said with a little apprehension as he continued to stare.

Buck saw the minute Dillon realized who he was. "Hello, faggot," he said. "I'll bet you weren't expecting me."

Buck saw Ian looking around, he presumed for a way out or a weapon of some sort. But before Dillon could make a break for it, Buck rushed him and attempted to jab the syringe into his neck.

Dillon's cell phone went flying through the air as he blocked Buck's arm, and the syringe went sailing after it.

"Fuck," Buck hissed as Dillon swung at him. He ducked just in time, avoiding the blow, and then threw a right hook of his own at Dillon.

But Dillon was quick on his feet as well. He dodged the hook, turned, and bolted for the steps. Buck ran after him and, before Dillon reached the stairs, Buck threw himself on top of the man and the two of them hit the floor with a thud. Dillon squirmed under him, but even forty pounds lighter, Buck still had at least sixty pounds on the guy. Buck reached into his top pocket and removed another syringe, and before Dillon could make a move, he jabbed it into Dillon's neck and pushed the plunger as hard as he could until it stopped.

BUCK STEVENS? Ian asked himself. *Could that really be Stevens? And if so, what in the fuck is he doing here? It's got to be him, and the fucker just jabbed something into my neck.* Ian struggled to get away, but he was suddenly so tired. His mind was getting cloudy, and he couldn't think. The numbness started in his feet and started working its way up his calves, rendering him paralyzed. Then it worked its way up to his knees and thighs, up his back to his neck and down his arms all the way to the tips of his fingers. *What's happening to me?*

The room was spinning, and Ian thought he might throw up, but he didn't have the energy to heave. Suddenly everything started to fade away. His last thought before everything went black was *Billy was right. Something wicked this way comes.*

Chapter Eight

BILLY AND his dad returned from fishing, and Billy started washing down the boat while his dad cleaned their catch of the day. Billy's phone started ringing, so he stopped and dried his hands before answering, feeling certain it was Ian. But when he glanced at the caller ID, it was Stella.

"Hi, Stella."

"Billy? Is Ian with you?"

"No," Billy said. "He's at the Royal Street house meeting the inspector."

"No, he's not," Stella said. "The inspector just called and said there's an SUV in the parking space and the keys are still in it, but Ian is nowhere to be found."

Billy looked at his watch. "I don't know what time he left, but he said he was meeting the inspector at eleven o'clock."

"Maybe he walked to a café or something to get something to eat and lost track of time," Stella suggested.

"No," Billy said. "Ian would never do that. He's as prompt as the bill collector." Dread filled him. He'd been waiting for the other shoe to drop, and here it was, hitting the floor with a great big *thud*. "I'm on my way to the Royal Street house now."

Billy's dad had stopped cleaning the fish and was eyeing Billy with a frown. "Son?"

"Dad," Billy yelled. "I need to borrow your truck. Something's happened to Ian."

"Of course," John said promptly. "But I'm coming with you. Your mom's out shopping, so I'll leave her a note and meet you in the garage."

On the hour-long drive into New Orleans, Billy filled his dad in on everything he knew.

"Dad," Billy said, "I've been having this weird feeling for the last few days that something bad was going to happen."

"Now let's not jump to any conclusions, Son. Maybe it's all just a big misunderstanding."

"No, Dad, I can feel it. Something's wrong with Ian."

"Okay, Billy," John said. "We'll figure this out."

When they finally reached the house, Billy pulled up to the gate and pressed in the same code he'd heard Stella mumble yesterday. The gate opened, and he drove down the narrow alley. Billy parked behind their rented SUV and a pickup truck with a sign on the door that said Vieux Carré Home Inspections. Before they entered the courtyard, Billy and John searched the SUV for any clues that might explain Ian's whereabouts. As Stella had mentioned, the keys were still in the ignition, but Billy saw nothing out of the ordinary.

"Nothing on this side, Son. Anything on yours?"

"Not a thing here either, Dad."

Billy led his father through the courtyard and into the house. There was no sign of anyone on the first floor. Billy prayed as he ran up the stairs that this would all be a misunderstanding and Ian was with the inspector now. The second floor was also empty. Billy listened and heard movement overhead. His heart raced as he ran up to the third floor, hoping to see Ian. But instead all he saw was a short, chubby man wearing a T-shirt with the same logo as he'd seen on the truck parked outside, climbing down a ladder from the roof rafters.

"This place is in great shape," he said. "Solid as a rock."

"I'm sorry, but are you alone?" Billy asked.

"I always work alone," the man said. "I'm Cecil Handers." When he reached the floor and got a look at Billy, he did a double take. "Hey, you're that country singer Billy Eagan. Me and my wife are big fans!"

"No!" Billy said. "I mean… yeah, I'm Billy Eagan, but has anyone else been here since you arrived?"

"No, sir. I was supposed to meet a Mr. Dillon here, but he never showed up," Cecil explained. At that point the lightbulb evidently went off in his head. "Mr. Dillon. That's your partner, right? The guy from the *National Intruder*? That was damn wrong what they done to you boys. Whose business is it anyway who you sleep with? Anyway, since the place was unlocked, I just went ahead with the inspection."

Billy rubbed his forehead. *Shit! Where is he?*

"Something wrong, Mr. Eagan?" Cecil asked.

"I don't know," Billy said. "Look, I'm sorry about this. I need to go. Just send the report to the Realtor, would you? Thanks, Cecil."

Without waiting for an answer, Billy went back down to the second floor. He was aware of his father following him down, but all he could think about was Ian. He went to the french doors and paced back and forth. Something on the floor caught his eye. He walked over and saw a syringe lying on the floor. He went to pick it up and then stopped. *Don't touch it, Billy!*

"Dad!" Billy yelled. "Look at this."

John hurried over and bent down next to the syringe. "It's still full, Son."

"Dad, Ian and I walked every inch of this building yesterday, and that syringe was not there," Billy said to his father. "I'm calling the police. Something is not right here. Ian's in trouble, I can feel it."

John quartered the room with his eyes and stiffened. Billy followed his father's gaze and spotted a cell phone lying faceup on the floor in the corner next to the window. As he took a closer look, his heart sank. It was Ian's.

Billy dialed 911 and explained the situation to the operator. She told him she would send someone over to file a missing persons report, but nothing could really be done until the person was missing for at least twenty-four hours.

"Twenty-four hours?" Billy snapped.

He started to argue with the woman but knew in the end it would do him no good. He would wait for the uniformed officer to show up, and then he would use whatever good will his celebrity would offer him to get the ball rolling sooner.

While he waited for the officer to show up, he called Josh. "Josh, it's Billy."

"Billy! How's the vacation going?"

"Josh, Ian's missing."

"What do you mean missing?"

Billy explained the situation, and thank God, Josh knew Ian well enough to know he wouldn't pull something like this. He agreed with Billy that something wasn't right.

"They're telling me they can't do anything for twenty-four hours. Can you call Mike and see if he has any connections here in New Orleans who might speed this investigation along?"

"Let me make a few calls," Josh said.

At that moment a uniformed police office tapped on the front window.

"I've gotta go, Josh. The police just showed up. Please, hurry."

"I'm on this, Billy."

Since Billy didn't have a key to any of the security locks the real estate agency had placed on the empty dwelling, he went to the window and explained to the officer through the glass how to get around to the gate. He met the guy there a few moments later.

The shock on the officer's face told Billy the man recognized him, and for once he was happy about that.

Billy stuck out his hand. "I'm Bil—"

"Billy Eagan," the officer said, finishing Billy's sentence. "I'm a big fan."

"Thank you very much. And your name is?"

"Oh, sorry. NOP—I mean, Boudreaux," the man said, nervously referring to his name badge. "Officer Paul Boudreaux *with* the NOPD."

"Officer Boudreaux," Billy said calmly. "I know you can't open this case until someone has been missing for at least twenty-four hours, but this is my partner we're talking about. His name is Ian—"

Officer Boudreaux finished his sentence once again. "Dillon. Ian Dillon."

"That's right," Billy said.

103

Officer Boudreaux leaned in close. "My husband, Roy, and I have been together for nine years."

Yessss. What are the odds?

"Roy and I are so happy you guys made your relationship public. It helps us all, you know."

"Thanks. But can we get back to Ian?"

"Oh sure, sorry."

Billy explained the situation once more, showed the officer the syringe and Ian's cell phone, assured him they hadn't touched either, and explained a little about Ian to assure the officer Ian hadn't just gone out for a sandwich.

Officer Boudreaux listened intently, and when Billy finished, he spoke. "You're correct about the 'twenty-four hour' situation. But in this case, there are extenuating circumstances. Are you absolutely sure the syringe wasn't already here?"

"I'm sure," Billy said, willing Boudreaux to believe him. "We walked all over the house. And what about the phone?"

"All right, I'll tell you what I'll do," Boudreaux said. "I'll escalate this up to one of our detectives, or better yet, to our Chief, and explain the situation. That ought to get the ball rolling."

Billy pumped the officer's hand. "Thank you. I'd really appreciate that."

Billy watched Boudreaux step into the courtyard to make the call. He couldn't make out Boudreaux's words, and the waiting was killing him. The more time that passed, the worse shape Ian could be in. John, who had remained silent while Billy interacted with the policeman, came over to stand beside him and laid a hand on Billy's shoulder. The quiet support helped—a little.

The officer finally came back when he finished his conversation. "This is weird, but the Chief got a call a few minutes ago about this same investigation."

Josh and Mike.

"Apparently they are sending over our top two detectives to get on this right away."

Mildly relieved, Billy glanced at his dad and tried to smile, but worry wiped the expression off quickly, and he sighed instead.

"You'll be in very good hands," Boudreaux assured him. "Is there a code to that security gate?"

"Four, two, four, two," Billy said, following the officer into the courtyard.

"Okay. I'll call Detective Hebert and pass that along so they can get in."

"I don't know how to thank you," Billy said.

"Just doing my job," Boudreaux replied. Looking a bit sheepish, he added, "But maybe the next time you have a concert in New Orleans, you could let me know?"

"Give me your card," Billy told him, "and I'll be sure you get front-row seats."

"That would be great," Boudreaux said, handing Billy his contact information. "Good luck, Mr. Eagan. I'm sure Mr. Dillon will turn up."

"Billy. Please. And I sure hope so. Thanks for everything."

The officer exited the way he came in, and Billy turned to his father. "Call me a whore," he said, "but when it comes to Ian, I'll do whatever it takes to get the job done."

"Whore away and do anything you have to do," John said. "I don't blame you one bit, Son."

Ten minutes later Billy and his dad were sitting in the courtyard, and Billy heard the security gate opening. He jumped up and ran to the parking area. A black unmarked Ford was slowly making its way up the alley, and Billy waved them in. The two men exited the car and introduced themselves.

"I'm Lead Detective August Hebert with the NOPD."

"And I'm Detective Bruce Jenkins."

"I'm Billy Eagan, and this is my dad," Billy said, gesturing to his father, "John Eagan."

"Pleased to meet you both," Detective Hebert said. "And can I just say, I'm a huge fan."

"Thanks," Billy said.

Detective Hebert looked around. "We've been told there seems to be some sort of a missing person issue going on here."

"Yes, sir. My partner, Ian Dillon, is missing."

Scotty Cade

"For how long now?" Detective Jenkins asked.

"About four hours now," Billy explained. "He was supposed to meet the building inspector here this morning at eleven o'clock. He left my parents' house on the North Shore around nine thirty. And his SUV is here, keys still in it, but he didn't show up for the appointment."

"I see," Jenkins said.

"And...," Billy continued as he led them into the house and up the stairs, "we found this"—referring to the syringe—"and I'm certain that's Ian's cell phone over there in the corner. I guarantee you Ian had that phone with him this morning, and the syringe wasn't here yesterday. We just bought this place and we went over every inch of it yesterday."

Detective Hebert stooped down and looked closely at the syringe. "It's not that uncommon to find a syringe in an abandoned building in the French Quarter. But... one that is still full of the contents is quite uncommon."

Hebert pulled a handkerchief out of his pocket and lifted the syringe, handing it to Jenkins, who was already waiting with a protective bag. Hebert bagged the cell phone next. "We'll run the prints on both of these right away and see what we come up with. Bruce!" Hebert yelled. "Get a crew over here to run this place, and let's see what we come up with."

"I'm on it," Jenkins said, reaching for his cell phone.

"Mr. Eagan," Hebert said.

"Please, call me Billy,"

"Okay, Billy. I know you guys have been getting a lot of publicity lately for coming forward with your relationship, but do you think all the attention could have been a little too much for Mr. Dillon?"

"Absolutely not," John chimed it. "Ian and Billy are the happiest I've ever seen them."

Detective Hebert looked at Billy.

"My dad's right," Billy agreed. "We've been together for five years, and as I said, we just bought this place yesterday. We're very happy."

106

"Okay, forgive me," Hebert said, "but I have to ask the tough questions."

"I get it," Billy said. "And I appreciate that. But I can assure you, Ian did not run."

"So," Hebert said, "Detective Jenkins and I are gonna get this syringe and phone down to the lab, have them check for prints, and do an analysis on the contents of the syringe. In the meantime, I have a crew on their way to sweep this place. Any evidence or lack thereof we find will determine whether we can do anything else until the twenty-four hour period has passed."

"I appreciate everything you're doing," Billy said.

Hebert nodded, dug for his wallet, and handed Billy a business card. "Here's a card for a private investigator friend of mine. He used to be a lead detective with the force, then he and his partner went out on their own and started their private investigation company. He's a good guy, and unlike us with our rules and protocols, they can get started ASAP."

Billy looked at the card and immediately recognized the logo. Bissonet and Cruz, Private Investigators.

"These guys are over on Magazine Street, right?"

"As a matter of fact they are," Hebert said.

"Our Realtor's office is right next door, and I remember being mesmerized by the nostalgic feeling of their building."

"That's what they were going for," Hebert agreed. "Beau and Tollison have a certain flair for nostalgia."

"I'll give them a call right away," Billy said, thanking the detective for the referral.

"All right, gentlemen," Hebert said. "Let me get this syringe and phone to the station, and I'll be in touch."

"Thank you so much," Billy said, pumping the officer's hand.

"Billy," John said. "You call the private investigators, and I'll show the detectives out."

Billy nodded. He called the number on the card and waited while the phone rang. He saw his father talking to the detectives and heard his muffled voice as someone picked up on the other end of the line.

"Bissonet and Cruz, Private Investigators. This is Iona Ball."

Iona Ball? Really? "Ah, good morning, Iona," Billy said politely. "Is Investigator Bissonet or Cruz in please?"

"Certainly, sir. May I ask who's calling?"

"My name is Billy Eagan."

A few seconds of silence on the line. "*The* Billy Eagan?" Iona asked.

"Yes, ma'am."

"Oh, Mr. Eagan, I'm such a big fan of yours, and I'm so happy for you and your partner."

"Ah… thank you, ma'am. The investigators?"

"Oh, certainly, sir. Sorry."

"No problem," Billy said. "This is sort of an emergency."

"Oh, yes, sir. Hold on while I transfer you."

Billy listened to the on-hold music. "As Time Goes By" from the movie *Casablanca* played in his ear.

How appropriate.

Right as Billy was on the verge of slipping back in time himself, the music abruptly ended, and he heard a man's deep voice. "This is Beau Bissonet. How can I help you?"

"Mr. Bissonet. My name is Billy Eagan, and I need your help."

"That's what we're here for," Beau said. "What can we help you with?"

Billy explained the situation and gave Investigator Bissonet a little background on Ian to make sure he didn't think Ian had bolted on him as well.

"Give me the address, and my partner and I will be right over."

Billy recited the address and the gate code to Bissonet and made a mental note that, when this was all over, they sure as hell needed to change the security code. "I'll be waiting, and please hurry," Billy said as he ended the call.

"Dad," Billy said. "Why don't you go on home and be with Mom? I'm sure she's freaking out, and there's no use in the both of us standing around here waiting."

"No way, Son, I'm not leaving you alone here."

"Dad, there's nothing you can do, and I don't want to have to worry about Ian and Mom both."

His dad gave him a defeated look, and Billy felt bad, but he really needed some time alone. And he surely didn't want to break down in front of his father if that's where this was headed.

"Okay, Son. If that's what you want."

"I just need a little bit of time alone to process all of this," Billy explained.

Before his dad could leave, the crime scene investigators showed up and started doing their thing.

"See," Billy said. "I won't be alone. It's gonna take these guys a while to do their job. I'll see you at home later."

As the crime scene guys bustled about doing their job, Billy walked his father to his truck.

"Are you sure?" John asked again.

"I'm sure, Dad," Billy said, giving his father a squeeze on the shoulder. "I promise I'll be fine."

In all actuality, it didn't take the crew long at all. They ran prints on all the interior and exterior doorknobs, window latches, and handrails going up and down the stairs. The place was gutted, so there really weren't any other surfaces to brush. Lastly they ran the SUV, then packed up and left.

Billy sat on the floor, his arms wrapped around his knees and his head resting on his arms. *This is all my fault. I shouldn't have allowed Ian to come here alone. If I had been with him, none of this would have happened.*

It was taking every inch of self-control he had to keep from falling apart. He raised his head when he heard footsteps. He brushed at his eyes in case any tears had escaped and got to his feet as two men entered the building from the courtyard. Both were about six feet tall; one had blond hair, was thickly built and ruggedly masculine, and had very pouty lips. The other was thinner and a little bit taller, with dark hair and dark eyes. He looked to be of Latin-American descent and was nicely dressed and, well... pretty. *Oh crap! A bubba and a pretty boy, that's all I need!*

109

The blond reached Billy first and stuck out his hand. "Beau Bissonet," he said. "And this is my partner, Tollison Cruz."

Billy shook both their hands. "Please help me" was all he could get out before the first tear slid down his cheek.

"We'll do our best," Tollison told him, resting a hand on his shoulder.

"Mr. Eagan," Bissonet said, "you told me the facts of the case over the phone, and I get all that, but what are your thoughts about Mr. Dillon's disappearance?"

"I don't know," Billy said. "Ian and I just went public with our five-year relationship, and everything went exceptionally well, except I've been having this feeling that everything has gone *too* well. We expected a little backlash, but nothing. And so I guess I've been waiting for a bomb to explode, so to speak. And boy has it."

"Let's not jump to any conclusions," Cruz said. "You know it's a different time now, with gay rights and marriage accepted in so many states. I think most of the country knew it was inevitable, so they simply accepted it and are on to the next thing."

"Yeah," Bissonet added. "It took me a good while to be accepted at the station, but it quickly became old news when a couple of detectives were caught having an affair and the married female officer popped up pregnant."

"You're gay?" Billy asked.

"As a goose," Beau said with a smile. "And not only is Tollison my business partner, he's my life partner as well."

"Well, I'll be damned."

"So you see, Mr. Eagan—"

"Please, call me Billy."

"Okay, Billy," Beau said. "You don't have to hold anything back."

"I'm not," Billy said. "I've told you everything I know. Ian and I are extremely happy."

"Okay," Cruz asked. "What about this syringe you mentioned?"

"It was over there on the floor." Billy gestured over his shoulder. "And it wasn't there yesterday. And... it was still full of whatever the hell was in it."

"The fact that it was still full could mean there was a struggle and the syringe was somehow knocked away from the scene and was never used," Bissonet speculated. "Did the police take it to the lab?"

"Yes," Billy said. "Detectives Hebert and Jenkins took it."

Beau looked at Tollison. "Auggie and Bruce?"

"August.... Yeah, Auggie, I guess."

"Auggie was my former partner," Beau said. "And Bruce was my former life partner."

"Oh geez," Billy said, rubbing his eyes. "This is getting confusing."

"Not really," Beau said. "Auggie and I were partnered on the force for many years. He's married with a couple kids. Bruce and I met when we were both still walking the beat. And he cheated—"

"Enough of your life story, Beau," Cruz interrupted with a slap to his arm. "Billy wants to find his partner, he doesn't need your gay history report from ancestry.com."

"Oh, sorry," Bissonet said. "You're right."

Beau looked around. "There's not a lot here, so we can't tell if there was any type of struggle. What about the courtyard or Mr. Dillon's car?"

"Nothing," Billy said. "The keys were still in the SUV, but it looked untouched and so did the courtyard." Billy felt himself starting to lose it. "What if some crazed homophobic fan of mine followed us here, took Ian, and is doing God knows what to him?"

"There's always that possibility," Beau said. "Ouch!"

Billy looked up to see Cruz jabbing Bissonet in the ribs.

"What I was gonna say right up until the time I was attacked," Bissonet said, casting an evil glance at Cruz, "was that while the scenario you describe is a possibility, it is highly unlikely."

"He's right," Cruz said. "Normally if someone is going to do something of this nature, they will profess their undying love in the form of a letter or social media post, tell you how much you hurt them, and then give you the opportunity to renounce your love of Mr. Dillon publicly. Next they will threaten Mr. Dillon's life or

111

yours before anything ever happens. Rarely do fans act on their threats, but it does happen from time to time."

Billy didn't know if he should feel better or worse with this new information.

"In most cases like this," Bissonet said, "it's usually someone that one of the two of you, or both of you, knows. Someone you've had issues with in the past, or someone who feels you wronged them in some way. Anyone like that ring a bell?"

"Oh God," Billy said. "Buck Stevens."

Cruz pulled out a small notepad from his inside coat pocket and started making notes.

"Who is this Buck Stevens?" Bissonet asked.

"Buck was a hand at a ranch I used to work on during my early days in Nashville, before my career took off," Billy explained. "I applied for a foreman position I saw in the paper, and unbeknownst to me, Buck had applied for the same position. I got the job, and he was pissed off."

"That's hardly a reason to go after Mr. Dillon," Cruz said. "Especially after all these years."

"That's only the beginning," Billy said. "Buck's girlfriend, Tina Roth, was a singer. She competed against me in an open mic contest and lost."

"And let me guess," Bissonet asked. "You won?"

Billy nodded. "Buck thought this girl was going to be his meal ticket, so again he was majorly pissed off. The more my career seemed to be taking off, the worse he treated me. One evening he lured me back to the ranch, hit me over the head with a baseball bat, and dragged me to an abandoned supply cabin on the lower acreage of the ranch. When I came to, I was tied to a bed next to his girlfriend. Buck set the place on fire and walked out.

"Luckily Ian and the ranch owner figured out something was up, made a beeline for the ranch, and saved us both. But Buck escaped and the police never found him."

"Holy fuck," Bissonet said. "That's where we start, Tollison."

"Got it," Cruz said over his shoulder as he turned and walked to a corner of the room. "I'll call Iona and get her to start a preliminary search to see what we can dig up."

"Meanwhile," Bissonet said, "I'll call Auggie to fill him in and see if they have any results from the syringe."

"Oh," Cruz said, turning around and walking back up to Billy. "I almost forgot. Here's our standard contract. Read it over, sign it, and get it back to us as soon as possible."

"Give me a pen," Billy said, opening the document and flipping to the last page.

Cruz handed him a pen and Billy signed it and gave it right back to Cruz.

"Aren't you gonna read it first?" Bissonet asked.

"I don't care what it says, I just want Ian back."

"We're on it, and we'll be in touch as soon as we know anything," Cruz said. "Now I need to call our assistant."

"Thank you, Mr. Bissonet," Beau said.

"Beau and Tollison to you, Billy," Bissonet said. "Stay strong, and we'll do the best we can to bring Ian back to you. I'll call you by the end of the day to let you know if we've made any progress."

Bissonet and Cruz left, and Billy was again alone in the last place Ian was known to have been. He climbed to the second floor, sat down, and leaned his back against the wall. *Who knows how many hours to go until the police will start their investigation,* he thought. *At least I have Bissonet and Cruz working on it now.*

How odd that these guys know the detectives, and their agency just happens to be in the same building I was so taken with on Magazine Street. "That has to be a good sign," Billy said out loud. "Hold on, Ian, baby, I'm coming for you."

"FUCK!" BUCK yelled, slapping himself in the forehead. "I can't believe I left that other syringe on the floor," he said to himself. "Damn! Everything happened so fast."

Buck hadn't expected Dillon to put up a fight, the fucking fag in his expensive clothes, and when the scuffle broke out and the syringe went flying, Buck had simply grabbed the second one and finished the job. As soon as Dillon hit the floor, Buck scooped him up, tossed him over his shoulder, and carried Dillon down the stairs to his truck. The problem was, he'd been in such a hurry to get out of there before the inspector showed up, he'd forgotten to go back and get the first syringe.

Buck's mother's voice kept ringing in his ears. "You were the biggest mistake of my life."

"And she was right," Buck said to himself. "You're a stupid motherfucker who can't get anything right."

Buck looked down at Dillon, who lay on the tabletop where Buck had placed him. He was still out cold, and Buck took the opportunity to study him before he secured him to the table. He'd tried to fight his impending erection as he'd begun to undress Dillon, but he'd eventually given up, not willing to take another punch to the balls. Besides, it was him and Dillon. No one else would ever know. And Dillon would never have the chance to tell. Buck was experiencing some kind of power trip, as well as a thrill anticipating being able to study the man's naked body when he was unable to protest.

He pulled Dillon's boots off one at a time, then unfastened his jeans and slowly slid them down. He studied the man's muscular legs and the bulge in Dillon's underwear.

The feeling of absolute control was growing stronger, as was Buck's erection. He fought to keep his hand away from his cock as he released the buttons on Dillon's shirt slowly, one by one. When Dillon's well-defined chest was completely exposed, Buck slipped Dillon's arms through the sleeves and pulled the shirt free, tossing it to the floor. He touched Dillon's nipples, pinching the little bulbs between his fingers, and then he bent down, and for the first time in his life, of his own accord, tasted another man's skin. He ran his tongue down Dillon's chest and stomach to the small patch of curly hair above his navel.

He pulled Dillon's socks off, tossed them aside, and stared down at the last piece of Dillon's clothing remaining: his underwear.

In Buck's mind this was the point of no return. But his sense of control seemed to be waning; he was losing his power to manage

114

his own actions. It was like he was under some sort of spell, being driven by an odd force other than his own will, and he was grudgingly giving in to it.

He hesitantly leaned down, placed his nose at Dillon's crotch, and inhaled deeply, breathing in a strong, masculine scent that made his cock twitch inside of his pants. He reluctantly brushed his nose against Dillon's bulge, then without a second thought put his entire mouth over Dillon's crotch and sucked in a ragged breath. Buck's cock twitched again, and he felt his orgasm start to build. Unable to stop himself, Buck yanked Dillon's underwear down to his ankles and completely off. Breathing heavily, he gazed at the totally naked man in front of him.

After staring at Dillon's limp cock for what seemed like forever, the unknown force insisted he take it into his mouth and taste it. How different it all seemed with no hand behind his head, forcing him down and making him gag. He took his time and savored the experience as he moved his mouth up and down the flaccid cock. He slid his fingers down to Dillon's balls and played with them as he continued to move his mouth up and down. Unconsciously he slipped his finger down a bit farther and stopped when he felt Dillon's moist opening. Buck's finger circled the opening a few times and then he brought his finger to his nose. The musky scent had Buck turning Dillon over onto his stomach to give him better access.

Buck spread the round globes of Dillon's ass and gazed upon the opening he'd just fondled. He gently touched the area around it, exploring the soft pinkish skin. He fought the urge to push his finger inside; that was for later, when Eagan was watching.

Dillon stirred a little, and Buck pulled back, but Dillon quickly settled again.

Buck had visions of climbing onto Dillon's back and having his way with the man, but again, he wanted Eagan here to witness the entire scene before he did away with them both.

Instead Buck unfastened his jeans and pushed them, along with his underwear, down to his ankles. He spit into his palm, took his own length in hand, and started to pump. He bent over Dillon's ass, inhaled that musky scent again, and imagined how it would feel when he finally took the plunge. Visions of Dillon screaming and trying to get away, like Buck had done as a kid, appeared in his head and drove his excitement to the verge. He screamed into Dillon's ass when he came into his own hand.

The minute his orgasm subsided, Buck regretted giving in to his desires. He cursed himself and retrieved Dillon's shirt from the floor, then wiped off his hands and cock with the garment and tossed it into the corner. Buck pulled his underwear and pants back up and kicked the table in a fit of anger. "You fucking queers," he screamed to the heavens. "You're all recruiters. Leave. Me. The. Hell. Alone."

Dillon stirred again. The drugs were obviously starting to wear off. Buck secured Dillon's hands together under the table, spread the man's legs apart, and tied his ankles to the table legs. As an added precaution, he used a roll of duct tape to secure Dillon's midsection to the table until Dillon was virtually unable to move a muscle.

IAN WAS back in his junior year of college at Bob Jones University in Greenville, South Carolina. He and his first love Todd Slocum were on spring break and visiting their parents. They were in the throes of passion in Todd's childhood bedroom when the door flew open and Todd's parents walked into the room. The look of hurt and betrayal on their faces was evident and beyond what Ian could have ever imagined. Todd jumped up and found his underwear and began to speak. At the raising of his father's hand, Todd stopped midsentence. Ian watched in horror as Todd's father came to the bed, yanked Ian out of it, and tossed him unceremoniously to the floor. "Now get dressed and get out," he yelled. "And never show your face in this house again."

Ian got dressed and fled the room, casting one last glance at Todd before fleeing. He knew Todd's parents would call his folks. His only hope was to get home and explain before his parents got the call. He drove frantically, but when he walked in the front door, his parents were waiting for him. Ian listened as his parents told him how humiliating it was to hear the Slocums tell them things about their son, things that went against everything they believed in, everything they had taught him. They told him he made their stomachs turn. They didn't give him a chance to speak; they told him to pack his bags and get out. As far as they were concerned, they no longer had a son, and he could kiss his family and his education good-bye.

Ian tried to explain that he and Todd were in love, but his father accused him of being delusional. Shocked, Ian asked what the Slocums had told them. As he stood there listening to his father recount the story, Ian couldn't believe his ears. The Slocums had told them they'd caught him raping their son. Ian began to weep as they told him Todd had placed his hand on the family Bible and sworn Ian was blackmailing him. They explained that Todd had confessed Ian had first raped him after a frat party, when he was intoxicated and couldn't defend himself. After that, Ian had threatened to tell Todd's parents he was gay and get him kicked out of school if he didn't continue to have sex with Ian. They also told his parents if Ian left town immediately and never contacted Todd ever again, they wouldn't press any formal charges.

Ian was horrified. He fell to his knees and pleaded with his parents to hear him out. "That's not the way it happened at all," he begged. "Please, listen to me."

But they refused. Their words echoed in his head. *Go away and never come back, or face prison time. You might be lucky enough to evade prison, but prison would be nothing compared to the fires of hell, and one day, that's where you will end up for eternity.*

Abruptly Ian was in his and Billy's bedroom, confessing the story to Billy.

"Oh my God, Ian," Billy said as he sat down on the bed and surrounded Ian with his arms.

Ian was unable to stop his tears from flowing. "My world had fallen apart in less than two hours. All that Todd and I had acknowledged—the love I thought would last forever—Todd had given it all up to save his damn education and his inheritance. My life was over. I had no family, no education, and about eighteen hundred dollars in my savings account. So I did as I was told. I left my life and my first and only love, vowing never to let anyone have the opportunity to hurt me again."

Billy held on to Ian until Ian stood up, breaking the embrace.

"Now you know," said Ian. "Now you understand why I can never trust anyone ever again."

"Ian, that's the most heartbreaking story I have ever heard, and I can't begin to imagine the pain you were in, but I'm not Todd. I would never sell you out; I could never live with myself."

"It doesn't matter, Billy," Ian said. "My mind's made up."

"You can't be serious, Ian. You can't turn your back on me, on us."

"Billy, you promised that if I told you the story and I still wanted you to leave, you would leave. I also remember you once saying that you'd never break a promise to me. I want you to leave."

Ian watched as Billy stood up and walked to the closet. He was moving slowly, as if every step caused him pain. After he filled his leather bag with some of his things, he turned to go, but on the way out, he stopped in front of Ian, put his arms around him, gently kissed his neck, and said, "I love you."

As he approached the doorway, he stopped, turned, and said, "Don't worry about the rest of my things. I'll come by when I know you're not here and pack them up, and I'll leave my key on the kitchen counter." He stepped through and slowly closed the door behind him.

"No! Billy! Stop!" Ian yelled. "Please don't go." But the sound of the door closing reverberated through his haze.

And now Ian was in a life raft in the middle of the ocean with no land in sight. Dark clouds were hanging over his raft, and every few seconds lightning flashed, followed by a horrible cracking sound. The thunder roared continuously. Suddenly the skies opened, and the rain began to pelt his sunburned body. His raft was quickly filling up with water, and no matter how fast he bailed the water out, the tiny boat kept filling up again.

As the waves crashed against it, Ian's raft was about to sink. But in a flash of lightning, he saw Billy in a boat, heading in his direction. Billy was rowing frantically and calling his name, begging him to hold on. Billy was coming for him.

As more water filled the boat and it slipped below the surface, Ian clung to the side, kicking wildly to keep his head above the crashing waves. He waved as Billy got closer and closer, but just as Billy offered him an oar, a mammoth shark with Buck Stevens's face leapt out of the water and on top of Ian, sending him under. Ian fought with the shark and punched him in the face repeatedly, but nothing worked. The shark kept trying to drag him deeper, and its fins continuously slapped at Ian's face as it attempted to hold his head below the surface.

"Wake up, fairy," the shark said, slapping the left side of Ian's face.

Why is this shark calling me a fairy?

"Come on. It's time to wake up, pretty boy."

Pretty boy?

The voice was getting louder and louder. "Dillon! Wake up."

How does the shark know my name?

Ian opened his eyes, and all his struggling against the shark and the ocean stopped. Everything was blurry, and he was so cold. He couldn't feel his hands or his feet.

Am I dead?

If I am dead, it's awful cold in heaven. But I guess it beats the alternative.

"Come on, pansy," someone said. No, not a shark. "Wake the fuck up."

Ian blinked continuously, trying to clear his vision. As the blurred edges of the picture started to come into focus, Ian realized it wasn't a picture at all. It was a man's face, so close to his he could smell the man's vile breath.

Once Ian's brain acknowledged what he was actually seeing, his heart leapt into his throat, and fear and dread filled every fiber of his being. All the events started unfolding in his mind. Buck and the French Quarter house. The struggle. Buck on top of him, and finally darkness.

He must have drugged me.

Scotty Cade

Ian's first instinct was to run. He began thrashing around, kicking his legs and moving his arms, but to no avail. He could hardly feel any of his body, but what he could feel was secured tightly. His hands were bound together under whatever surface he was lying on—some sort of table?—and his legs appeared to be tied to its legs. When he looked up, he saw he was being held in some sort of enclosed space. The walls were silver, and there was a vented shelf against the wall opposite him. Then he looked over his shoulder and all hopes of escape faded. From his upper back down to his ass and his knees down to his ankles, he was secured to the table with silver duct tape.

"Are you satisfied now that you're not going anywhere?" Buck asked.

Ian dropped his head in defeat. Buck was right. He wasn't going anywhere. He was so consumed with despair, he wanted to fade back into the darkness. His only hope was that Billy was looking for him. But as his mind continued to clear, he suddenly realized if Billy came looking for him—and he knew he would—Billy could possibly end up in the same situation. Ian knew it was Billy Buck really wanted.

He's using me as bait! Oh God, Billy! Please stay away!

Chapter Nine

BILLY WATCHED as the sun worked its way across the cement floor of the French Quarter house until it eventually made it to the tiny corner in which he was huddled. His parents had called twice, wondering when he was coming home, and he'd kept telling them soon, but he couldn't pull himself away from the last place Ian had been. And besides, if he went home, it would be even worse. An empty guesthouse, an empty bed, and an empty existence.

Billy kept thinking if Ian was lost or confused for some reason, he might come back to the last place he remembered. But if no one was here, then he'd just keep moving. He knew the thoughts were irrational, but it was all he had. "Nope," he said to himself out loud. "I'm staying right here."

His phone rang again, and he looked at his caller ID. *Beau!*

"Beau," Billy said. "Please tell me you have news?"

"I do have some news," Beau replied. "I tracked down one Buckwald Bernard Stevens. His last known residence was Mount Juliet, Tennessee. But… he's wanted in Hiawassee, Georgia, for several outstanding parking tickets."

"Mount Juliet is where the ranch I told you about is located." *Oh my God. Jean and Jules. I completely forgot to call them.*

"Here's the thing, Billy. Tollison and I feel certain we have our man."

Billy stood and started pacing in front of the second-floor window. "How so?" he asked.

"We have at least three pictures of his expired license plate from the tollbooth of the Causeway, crossing from North Shore to Metairie over the last few days, the latest being this morning around 8:42."

Billy's heart fell to his stomach. His legs were about to give out, so he moved back against the wall and slid down to the floor.

121

"Oh God, no. He was following Ian," he said, resting his head on his knees.

"Now, Billy," Beau said. "Let's look at this logically. Tollison and I both agree that logically it's you Buck wants. He failed to kill you once, so this time he's using Ian as bait. If Buck has Ian, he will get in touch with you. Auggie has put a tracer on your phone, so when he does contact you, we can trace the call. And when he does call, I can guarantee you he will try to get you to meet him somewhere and maybe even try to extort money from you."

"I don't care about the money," Billy said on the verge of tears. "I'll give him everything we have. I just want Ian back."

"When he does contact you, you'll need to be smart about this, Billy," Beau explained. "He's more than likely gonna tell you that if you involve the police, he's gonna kill Ian, and he will most definitely tell you to come alone. Both of those are bad ideas. He won't kill Ian until he has you, and you will most definitely not be going alone. He may think you're alone, but we will most certainly be close by."

"I'm scared, Beau. This guy is a lunatic. We have no idea what he might do."

"Look," Beau said, "I've contacted Auggie and Bruce, and they've put out an arrest warrant for him. But even if we get him, unless his fingerprints are on that syringe, we can't hold him longer than twenty-four hours without proof that he kidnapped Ian."

"Okay," Billy said, the dread almost consuming him.

"One more thing," Beau said. "Fuck waiting for the lab reports. Auggie and Bruce and Tollison and I are on this now. They've put a rush on the syringe prints and have the crime scene investigators working nonstop on everything they collected. We're gonna get this guy."

"Thanks, Beau. I'll never forget this."

"Don't thank me until after you get my bill," Beau teased.

"I'm sure you guys are gonna be worth every penny," Billy mumbled.

"I'll be in touch," Beau said as he ended the call.

Billy heard movement, and for a split second, he thought Ian had found his way back home. But instead, he saw his mom and dad, Jean and Jules, and Josh and Suzie walking up the stairs.

Billy stood and wiped his eyes. Before he could walk over to greet them, Jean and his mom ran to him and threw their arms around him. With the support of the two women who meant the most to him in the world, he was finally able to let go. He sobbed endlessly, holding on for dear life while Suzie sobbed in Josh's arms and all the men seemed to be fighting back tears of their own.

When Billy could speak again, he apologized to Jean and Jules for not calling them, and they completely understood. Next he filled them in on Buck's whereabouts.

"He's in Louisiana?" Vicki asked.

"Apparently he followed us here from Tennessee and has been following us ever since," Billy explained. "They have a warrant out for his arrest, but Buck has evaded the authorities for all this time, so I'm not too hopeful. And unless his fingerprints are on that syringe, they can't hold him longer than twenty-four hours."

"This is all my fault," Jules said. "If I had fired that guy when I had the chance, none of this would have happened."

"No," Jean said, running to his side. "Coulda. Shoulda. Woulda. Stop it. This is no one's fault."

"Absolutely not," Billy said, walking over to Jules and wrapping his arms around him. "None of this is your fault."

"But—"

"No," Billy said. "This guy is crazy, and you firing him would have made no difference."

Before Billy could go on, his cell phone rang again. "It's Detective Hebert," he said. "Hey, Detective."

Hebert cleared his throat. "I know you talked to Beau, so I won't go over it again, but I wanted to let you know the fingerprints on the syringe are an exact match to Buckwald Bernard Stevens, and the cell phone is definitely Ian's. In addition, the lab reports came back, and the contents of the syringe was a mixture of diluted Xanax and Valium. Because of the dilution, there wasn't enough to kill him, but it was surely enough to put him out cold for four to six hours, depending on how big a guy Ian is."

Billy didn't know whether to be the tiniest bit relieved or remain scared to death. Ian was probably still alive, but Buck still had him. "Thanks, Detective. Please don't hesitate to call with any more news."

"If Buck is out and about, we'll find him," Hebert said. "Oh— a couple more things."

"Yes, sir," Billy replied.

"This may not even be related, but the library on St. Charles Avenue called in a concern about someone searching ways to sedate someone by injection or inhalation. And right after that search, the same person searched areas hardest hit by Hurricane Katrina."

"What does that mean?"

"Maybe nothing," Hebert said. "And maybe our guy was doing some homework."

"What were results of the search?" Billy asked.

"The last site he visited described what we found in the syringe."

"That can't be a coincidence, can it?"

"We don't know yet. We have someone heading over to the library to show the staff the last picture we have of Stevens. Maybe they can make a positive ID."

"What do the areas hardest hit by Katrina have to do with anything?" Billy inquired.

"Maybe our man is searching for a secluded place in which to hold Ian."

"And what did his search show?"

"Anyone who lives in NOLA could answer that without a computer. Chalmette and the Lower 9th Ward," Hebert said. "Those are the places he was looking at. And before you ask, I've sent several patrol cars to that area as well as alerted all patrols about what's going on."

"Thank you," Billy said.

"No thanks needed. Just doing our job. And the last thing is, so you'll know, Bruce Jenkins is holding a press conference in about an hour and a half. The best shot we have is the hope that someone has seen either Buck or Ian."

"Detective, can I please pass the phone to Josh Randal? He works for my record label, and my publicist needs to be kept in the loop. Not to interfere in any way, but so they can prepare the proper statements for the press. Once this gets out, it's gonna go big."

"I understand," Hebert said, "and I'll be glad to share our intentions with him."

Billy held out the phone. "Josh, they're doing a press conference soon, and I want to make sure Capitol is in the loop. Can you handle this?"

"Of course," Josh said, taking the phone and walking to the corner of the room.

"Now, Billy," Vicki said. "We've all discussed it, and you're coming home with us."

Billy opened his mouth to speak, but his mother interrupted him.

"There is nothing to keep you here any longer. They're gonna find Ian and bring him home, but we can't do any more from here. And besides, this place doesn't even belong to you yet."

Billy hadn't thought of that. They had a contract, but they hadn't closed. He bowed his head in defeat. "Okay," he said reluctantly. "I'll go."

Josh walked up to Billy and handed him his phone. "We're all set. On the way back, I'll call Mike and get the label in touch with your publicist, and together they can work up a statement. They'll send it to me so we can review everything before it's released."

"Thanks, Josh."

Josh wrapped his arms around Billy and held on tightly. "We'll find him, man," he whispered. "We'll find him."

On the ride back to the North Shore, John drove with Jules beside him in the passenger seat. Billy sat in the back with Jean on his left and his mother on his right, and Josh and Suzie were following in the rental.

The car was eerily silent as John drove across the Causeway. Jules and John both watched the road ahead, while Jean and Vicki stared out of their windows at the choppy waters of Lake

Pontchartrain. Billy also stared blankly at the road ahead while holding his phone tightly against his chest, willing it to ring. Beau had said Buck would call, but when? And how long would he need to keep Buck on the line for the police to be able to trace the call—assuming they could? When Buck did call, what would his demands be for the return of Ian? Deep down he knew the answer to that question, and he knew he would do whatever he had to do to assure Ian's safety. Even sacrifice his own life for Ian's—but he would keep that to himself.

The silence was interrupted when Billy's phone rang. Jean and Vicki both gripped his legs. Jules turned from the front seat and John looked at him in the rearview mirror. All eyes were on him as Billy's heart went into overdrive, his phone vibrating against his chest. He said a quick prayer before looking at the caller ID. *August Hebert.*

In a split second, a few different scenarios played out in his head: *They still have no news. They found Ian, and he's alive and well. They found Ian, and he's dead.*

"Hello," Billy said, his voice cracking.

"Billy. It's Detective Hebert," the voice said, void of any detectable emotion.

"Yes, sir," Billy replied shakily.

"I just wanted to give you an update."

Billy was unable to speak and remained silent.

"Billy?" Hebert asked.

"I'm here," Billy murmured.

"Oh, sorry! I thought I'd lost the call. Anyway, I have a tracer on your phone, so when Stevens contacts you, we can trace the call back to the closest cell tower and at least give us a general area to start searching."

Billy swallowed hard and willed himself to ask the question he had been considering himself. "How long do I have to keep him on the line for you to trace the call?"

"It used to be at least sixty seconds, but with today's cell phone technology, we can tell if he's stationary or moving by simply following the pings from the cell towers. It's instantaneous now. But

126

the longer you keep him on the line, the better chance we have at pinpointing his location, or where's he headed, depending on the type of phone he's using, of course."

Billy struggled to form words. "I'll do my best" was all he was able to say.

Hebert continued. "The press conference went well, and calls have started to come in. We used the latest picture of Stevens we could find, but we have no idea how his appearance has changed since that photo. We're hopeful since he's been in town as long as you have, someone will recognize him. Wait a sec. Just hang on, Billy."

Billy listened to Hebert's muffled voice as he imagined him covering the phone and speaking to someone in his office.

"Billy!" Hebert said. "We have our first lead."

Billy sat up straight and held his breath. "I'm listening."

"We just got a call from a Walmart on Chef Menteur Highway in the 9th Ward of New Orleans. The clerk said she thought she recognized the guy, but she couldn't be sure. He was thinner, completely bald, and had a beard. What clued her in was what the guy bought."

"And?" Billy asked.

Hebert sighed. "Syringes, duct tape, rope, a prepaid cell phone, and a fifth of bourbon."

"When you get to the next crossover, turn around and head to the 9th Ward," Billy said to his father. "Buck was spotted in a Walmart on Chef Menteur Highway buying syringes, duct tape, and rope."

"Wait," Hebert said. "Let us handle this, Billy."

"I can't just sit back and do nothing. The computer searches done at the library resulted in the same drugs found in the syringe, and the Walmart is in the Lower 9th Ward. He's got to be there."

"Billy," Hebert said, "he could have just as easily bought the syringes before he abducted Ian and gone all the way out there to throw us off his trail. It could be a dead end."

"I don't care," Billy said. "It's all I have to go on, and I can't sit around and wait. We're going."

Scotty Cade

"Billy," Hebert pleaded, "Beau and Tollison were here for the conference, and they're headed in that direction now, and I'm also sending a shitload of guys out there to see if they can pick up the trail. This is all nothing but a crapshoot until we get that call from Stevens. Whatever you do or wherever you go, make sure you stay in cellular range."

"Will do," Billy said with renewed hope as he disconnected the call.

John pulled into the first crossover, stopped, and rolled down his window. Josh pulled up beside him and did the same. "Buck has been spotted in a Walmart in the 9th Ward. We're heading back in that direction."

"No!" Billy shouted. "We're not heading back in that direction. I am."

John held up his hand. "Don't interrupt me when I'm talking." He looked back at Josh. "*We're* heading back in that direction."

"Not without me," Josh said.

"Hold on a second, Josh." John turned to look at Jean and Vicki. "I don't want this to sound sexist in any way, but this guy is dangerous, and if we find him, there's no telling what he might do. I think we can better focus on finding Ian if we don't have to worry about you ladies. Would you please consider going back to the house with Suzie and let us go find Ian?"

Vicki started to protest, but Jean reached across Billy and rested a hand on her forearm. "It's probably for the best," she said. "As much as I want to wrap my hands around Buck Stevens's neck and choke him until he turns purple for what he's done to our boys, I don't want Jules to have to worry about me."

Vicki closed her eyes and nodded. She took Billy's hand in hers and squeezed. "I love you, and I know you'll find Ian," she whispered. "But please, please be careful."

She kissed Billy on the cheek, got out of the car, and kissed John through the driver's side window. Jean kissed Billy on the other cheek and slid out of the car. Jean leaned in the passenger window and hugged Jules. "Be careful, and bring our boy home safely."

Hearing the sentiment in their voices almost brought Billy to tears. But he couldn't allow that to happen. Not now.

Billy watched as Josh said his good-byes to Suzie and then slipped in the backseat with him. John hit the accelerator and sped off in the other direction.

IAN WAS getting more and more alert as the drugs wore off and the hours progressed. He was cold, naked, thirsty, and he had to pee. Buck had been sitting in a chair staring at him, a look on his face that, if Ian didn't know any better, was pure lust. He had the bourbon bottle in his hand and was taking a shot every few minutes. Ian's only hope was that Buck would drink until he passed out and give him time to try and come up with a plan to break free.

"What are you looking at, faggot?" Buck said, his voice only slightly slurred.

Ian closed his eyes and tried to figure out how to answer. "I'm thirsty, and I have to pee," Ian said, avoiding the question altogether.

"Fuck you," Buck said. "I don't have any water, and you might as well go ahead and piss yourself now because you're never getting out of here."

Fucking great.

Ian decided to try and keep Buck talking. He didn't know why, but he'd seen that tactic on some detective show. So with no other ideas, he went with the thought. "What are you going to do with me?" he asked.

"Does it really matter?" Buck asked. "Neither you nor Eagan are getting out of here alive."

So he does plan on using me as bait for Billy. Keep him talking.

"But Billy's not here," Ian said calmly.

"He will be," Buck responded, tipping the bourbon bottle to his lips and taking another swig.

"How?" Ian asked.

Scotty Cade

Buck took the bottle away from his lips. "Oh, I think I'm just gonna give him a little more time to get more and more worried about you so he becomes frantic. That way when I call with my demands, he won't hesitate to meet them."

"Is it money you want?" Ian asked.

Buck roared with laughter. "Money is going to be part of it, but that's just a by-product of my plan. It's your boyfriend I really want."

"Come on, Buck," Ian pleaded. "What did Billy really do to you?"

Buck took another swig of bourbon. "Let's see," he said. "For starters he took my job and my meal ticket. Then if that wasn't bad enough, because you and that old fuck Jules James saved Billy and that bitch Tina from the fire and turned me in to the police, I've been on the run ever since."

"Buck," Ian said quietly, trying to engage the man in more conversation. "Billy didn't set out to hurt you. He answered an ad in the paper for a job."

"The job was bad enough," Buck said. "But when he beat Tina in the competition and made it big, that was the end of the line."

"If it hadn't have been Billy who beat her, it would have been someone else," Ian said. "She just wasn't good enough to be in the big time."

Buck didn't say anything right away. But he walked over to Ian and gazed at his naked body. He brushed a finger over Ian's cheek. "Isn't that sweet. You love your faggot boyfriend so much you're making excuses for him. I reckon he loves you back that much, don't he? Enough to make him come when I call. It must be nice to have someone love you that much."

"I'm not making excuses," Ian said. "It's the truth." And then he processed that last sentence: "It must be nice to have someone love you that much."

Buck never felt loved. How can I use that to my advantage? Keep him talking, Ian.

"Speaking of the end of the line," Buck asked. "How did you like the *National Intruder* story? Meet the anonymous source."

"So it was you," Ian said.

130

"Yep. It was me," Buck shared. "And it earned me a whopping ten grand."

Before Ian could speak, Buck lightly brushed the skin on the back of Ian's neck. He slid a finger down Ian's back and Ian shivered as Buck's finger moved along his spine. Ian held his breath when Buck continued down his back to the crack of his ass. He felt Buck's hand stop and linger there, circling his opening. Ian looked over his shoulder just in time to see Buck retrieve his hand, bring his fingers up to his nose, and inhale deeply.

That was *lust in his eyes.*

Buck took another swig of bourbon and continued to stare at Ian.

"Weren't you ever loved like that?" Ian asked, trying to keep the information coming. Anything he could use as ammunition against Buck later, some way to get into his head and confuse him with mind games.

Buck gave out a disgusted laugh. "Oh, I was loved alright, but it certainly wasn't that kind of love."

Ian was trying to fit the pieces of the puzzle into place as Buck gave up little bits of the picture here and there.

"Did your parents not love you when you were growing up?" Ian asked.

Ian watched Buck focus his gaze on something against the opposite wall, like he was reliving a painful memory.

"Buck?" Ian asked. "You want to talk about it?"

Ian's voice brought Buck out of whatever trance he was in. "Shut the fuck up, faggot," Buck said, kicking the table.

Ian closed his eyes and waited for what was coming next.

"I didn't think you queer recruiters did anything but look for warm holes to fuck. It's all about the warm hole, isn't it, fag? You're no better than my stepfather."

Buck crossed his right arm in front of his chest and let go with an elbow to Ian's head. "Yep! Just like him. We'll see how you like it being on the receiving end."

Buck's elbow hit Ian above the temple, and his head jerked to the side. He saw a bright flash of light and then his head exploded with pain. He was suddenly nauseous again, and his head was throbbing, but he didn't miss what Buck had said.

His stepfather sexually abused him as a kid.

Ian had a moment of pity for the poor bastard, but he couldn't afford not to use what he'd learned, and he jumped back in while the iron was hot. "Billy and I, we're not your stepfather, Buck," Ian said. "Whatever he did to you had nothing to do with us."

"You better shut up if you know what's good for you," Buck barked. "You may not *be* him, but you're just *like* him. All you fags are the same."

Buck sat back down in his chair and focused on that same spot on the opposite wall.

"I'm sorry," Ian said.

"For what?" Buck replied in an even tone.

"For what he did to you," Ian answered.

"You don't know anything about me," Buck hissed.

"I don't know it all, Buck, but I've picked up some from what you've said. And I think your stepfather abused you in some horrible way."

"Yeah, well," Buck said as he took another shot of bourbon and swallowed. "Shit happens. Now shut your fucking trap before I shut it for you."

"You didn't deserve it," Ian said, taking one more shot. "No kid deserves to be treated that way."

Buck walked over and Ian braced himself for what was coming. Buck reached up and Ian flinched. But instead of hitting Ian, Buck brushed Ian's hair back out of his face. "Like you think you don't deserve this," he said as he threw his fist into the side of Ian's head.

Ian saw another flash of bright light, and then everything went dark.

"OUCH," BUCK said, opening and closing his fist. "That queer's got a hard head."

The bourbon was starting to relax him and break down the walls that guarded his secret. He studied his naked prisoner. The width of his shoulders, his bulging biceps, the muscles down his back to his round, rock-hard ass and on down to his thighs and calves. When he looked back up at Ian ass, Buck's dick twitched again.

He decided he couldn't wait much longer for what he desired. He'd fuck Dillon again once Eagan was here to watch. But he certainly wasn't going to fuck Dillon while he was passed out. What good would it be with no screams or resistance? No, he would wait a little bit longer, but it was time to make the call. Buck smiled as he typed Billy's telephone number into the prepaid cell phone as Ian started moaning. While the phone connected, Buck patted himself on the back for being so smart and downed another shot of bourbon.

My mother was a fucking liar. I am one smart man. Keeping Eagan's cell phone number was a good move, and buying this prepaid cell? That was pure genius.

JOHN, JULES, Billy, and Josh sped down I-610 toward the Industrial Canal and St. Claude Avenue. Jules was on the phone with Tollison, getting directions to meet up with them, and Billy was on his phone listening as Beau explained what they were up against. Beau told him the Lower 9th Ward had been the hardest hit by Hurricane Katrina, and although they'd made major strides to rebuild, nine years later many of the houses were still abandoned. On a better note, he told Billy the area was technically less than five square miles, so they would start at the heart and work their way out. But Billy remembered Hebert's words: *This is all nothing but a crapshoot until we get that call from Stevens.*

But it was all he had to hold on to, so he was going to give it all he had.

They arrived at the meeting point in the Walmart parking lot on Chef Menteur Highway where Buck had bought his supplies.

Beau and Tollison were waiting for them. Hebert and Jenkins were inside interviewing the sales clerk again, and their guys were already driving through the streets looking for Buck's truck. But Beau and Tollison had their own plans.

"If I were Buck," Beau said, "I would find some inconspicuous deserted house, probably with a garage of some sort to hide the truck in, and hunker down. We need to search every vacant house in the area."

"We've divided the area up into six sections," Tollison added, making eye contact with Billy and the others. "Each of us will take a section. Everybody has a cell phone, I assume, so if you find anything out of the ordinary, call me or Beau. We'll call Hebert's crew and get them over there to investigate."

"That's important," Beau stressed. "I know you've all got a big stake in this, but it won't do Ian any good if you get yourself hurt. Leave the investigating to the pros."

Billy, John, and Jules took off in one direction, while Tollison, Beau, and Josh headed out in the other. As they drove, Billy was amazed at how much destruction had befallen this little area of town. The things Beau had told him really hadn't done the area justice. There were houses half off their foundations; abandoned lots overgrown with weeds and vines. There was even a barge still sitting in the middle of town, right where Katrina had left it.

John pulled up to Jules's designated area. Jules opened the car door and Billy put his hand on Jules's shoulder. "Jules, if you see anything out of the ordinary, call the guys first, but then call me immediately after. And… please be careful. I'd hate to have to face the wrath of Jean if you got injured."

Jules nodded as he slipped out of the truck. "I'll remember, and if he's here, Billy, we'll find him."

"Thank you," Billy said, his voice cracking.

When John got to Billy's area, Billy repeated the plan with his father as he got out of the truck. "Please be careful, Dad."

"You too, Son," John replied. "Like Jules said, if he's here, we'll find him."

Billy took out his cell phone to make sure he had a strong signal. *Four bars!*

He looked around to get his bearings and then started up the block. After forty minutes, he'd searched seven abandoned houses. So far he'd seen no sign of anything strange. He'd chatted with a couple of the neighborhood residents he ran across and asked if they'd seen anything unusual, but still nothing. He was about to start on house number eight when his cell phone rang. He fished it out of his pocket; he didn't recognize the number. His heart raced as he answered.

"Hello," Billy said hesitantly.

"Well, hello there, stranger."

Billy knew the voice instantly. "Buck! Where's Ian? It's me you want, so tell me where you are and I'll get there. Just let Ian go."

"Whoaaaa, Hoss!" Buck said. "Not so fast."

"Buck, Ian's done nothing to you."

"I wish I could say I hadn't done anything to him either. But sadly I cannot."

"Let me talk to him," Billy pleaded.

"He's, uhh… taking a little nap right now."

Billy's voice got stronger and louder. "Tell me where you are, Buck, and I'll come to you. I'm all yours."

"All in good time, Eagan. First you need to do a few things for me."

"Name it," Billy said anxiously.

"I want a half million dollars in small bills by six o'clock this evening. Then you, and you alone, will meet me at a designated location."

Billy looked at his watch. It was nearly three thirty. *Shit!*

"What else?" Billy asked.

"You come alone," Buck said. "If I even smell a cop, Ian dies. You got that?"

"I got it," Billy said forcefully. "Now if you want all this to happen as you described, I need to know Ian is still alive. So you either put him on the phone or we have no deal."

"I don't think you're in the driver's seat here, Hoss."

135

"I don't care who's fucking driving," Billy yelled. "Either I talk to Ian, or you get nothing."

"Ohhhh, fine," Buck teased. "Talk to your lover boy."

Billy heard some rustling sounds and Buck's muffled voice in the background. Then his heart almost leapt out of his chest when he heard Ian's voice.

"Billllly," Ian moaned.

"Ian, I'll find you. I'll always find you. Don't give up. I love you."

"Stay… away. He'll… kill… us both."

Billy heard a crack that sounded like bone against bone, and he fell to his knees. "You son of a bitch," he yelled into the phone.

"Oh calm down, sissy. He's just knocked out. He's quite the little chatterbox."

"So help me God, Buck! If you hurt him, I will hunt you down and torture you until you die from the pain."

Buck laughed out loud. "I'll look forward to it," he said. "Six o'clock. I'll be in touch."

"Wait—"

The phone went dead.

Billy called Beau and relayed the conversation, and Beau said he'd call Hebert and Jenkins. Then Billy called his dad and Jules. He again got his bearings and started running in the direction his father had driven.

His dad was there within five minutes, and they picked up Jules along the way and made a beeline for the Walmart parking lot.

"Good job, Billy," Hebert said when he got out of the truck. "He's using a prepaid cell phone, but you kept him long enough for us to get the necessary tower readings. We know he's stationary and in this area. Unless he took the battery out of his phone, we may be able to pinpoint his exact location. The precinct is working on that now."

"Jesus," Billy said. "I can't believe all this is happening."

"We're closing in," Hebert said. "And he has no idea."

"I'm sure Beau told you the entire conversation. Right?" Billy asked. "If he even suspects the cops are with me, he said he'd kill Ian. I want to go in alone."

"No way," Hebert said. "This is what we do. Trust me when I say we got this."

Ignoring Hebert's response, Billy asked, "How am I gonna get the money before six?"

"I have some counterfeit bills on the way," Jenkins volunteered. "This guy is not the sharpest tool in the shed, so he'll never know the difference."

"And what if he does?" Billy asked. "Guys, this is Ian's life we're playing with. Please don't do anything that's going to jeopardize it."

John, Josh, Jules, Beau, and Tollison were standing right behind Billy like his posse. When a hand landed on his shoulder, he turned to see his dad looking at him. "We have to trust them to do their job, Son."

"Like hell we do," Beau said as he left the group and headed straight for Hebert and Jenkins.

The three men argued, chests puffed out and voices raised, although Billy couldn't make out what was being said.

Finally Beau returned. "After reconsidering, Hebert and Jenkins have graciously agreed to have the NOPD hang back and allow Tollison and me to accompany you to the drop-off point. Out of sight, of course."

Billy nodded in relief. Two were better than a squad, but he was still not alone. He guessed it was a chance he would have to take. Or was it?

Hebert took a call and glanced over at Billy. As soon as he hung up, Billy approached him and asked, "Any luck with tracing the location the call came from?"

"Na," Auggie said. He couldn't seem to meet Billy's eyes. "He must have removed the fucking batteries from the phone."

"Maybe he's not as stupid as we thought," Billy replied.

"Or he watched too many crime shows on television," Hebert said. "I swear those CSI shows are exposing all of our secrets and single-handedly killing our investigation techniques."

Within the hour, Billy was wired with audio and a tracking device, and the money arrived. He inspected it; Hebert had been right. Billy couldn't tell the money wasn't real. He threw the bag into his dad's truck, reached under the seat where he knew his dad's .45 was hiding, and slipped it in the back of his pants.

Billy looked at his watch and paced back and forth. It was 4:40 and still no call from Buck.

"Guys," Billy said, "I just can't stand around here and wait. I'm gonna take a ride. Maybe I can still find him before this goes any further. I'll let you know as soon as the call comes in."

"Don't go far," Beau yelled.

"I won't."

Billy drove back in the direction he'd searched earlier. Buck's words kept going through his head. *If I even smell a cop, Ian dies. You got that?*

Billy decided he couldn't chance it. He pulled over to one of the houses he'd searched earlier, unbuttoned his shirt, and carefully removed the tracking device. He placed the wire inside the abandoned garage and climbed back in the truck. He drove block after block, looking for any signs, and waited for Buck's call.

AS SOON as Buck broke off the call from Billy, he went back to guzzling his bourbon and staring at Ian's naked body, imagining what he was going to do to it when Billy was finally there to watch. His thoughts were interrupted when his phone chirped. *Low battery?*

"Fuck," Buck whispered. "I forgot these things don't come fully charged."

Buck disconnected the battery and set it alongside the phone. All he needed was one more call and he could trash the whole damn thing.

His original plan had been to drug Billy with the last syringe when he arrived, wait for him to come around, and then do what he intended. But he wasn't sure he could stand to wait the four to six hours for Billy to come to, so he decided on another approach. A much quicker one that got him what he needed much faster.

IAN WAS on the verge of waking up, but horrible dreams kept pulling him back into darkness.

He was back in his old pickup truck, driving like a bat out of hell through the foggy and rainy South Carolina night. Tears blurred his vision, and the fog welled up around the truck thick as clouds, making it almost impossible to see the road.

Ian squinted, trying to make out the road ahead. Instead, faces began to drift out of the haze, pale and unnaturally elongated, but still recognizable.

His father, eyes burning with anger. His mother, features immobile as carved marble, no love, no mercy, nothing but contempt. Todd, lips stretched in a grin that nearly bisected his visage, gloating in triumph at the success of his betrayal.

Ian was no longer in control of the vehicle. It moved along slowly as if tethered to the faces in the mirk, drawn by the common goal of Ian's utter destruction.

The whispers began, although the spectres' mouths remained motionless.

Fires of hell, waiting for you.

Sick things. Such sick things.

Raped me. You raped me. Never loved you.

The truck sped up until it was flying down a road Ian couldn't see. And then it was flying over a roadside embankment into a suddenly clear blue sky. No faces, no voices, no fog. But the earth was rushing up to meet him, and Ian threw his arms over his face, waiting for the end...

And found himself sitting on a barstool, watching a tall, thin, mature, but very attractive woman approach from the far end of the bar.

"Welcome to Jean's Magnolia Saloon," she said, smiling at him warmly. "What can I get for you, sweetie?"

139

Jean. Her name was Jean. She knew everything about Ian because he had told her everything. All about his lover, Todd, who betrayed him, and his parents, who turned him out with nothing because he was gay. Jean was the mother he'd always wanted. She didn't hate him for being gay. She saved him, gave him a job, a home, then a career. Gave him his life back, gave him….

Billy. You can get me Billy. I need Billy.

"Billy?" she asked, although he was sure he hadn't spoken aloud. "Why of course, honey. He'll be up there onstage any minute now. Any… minute… now."

There, in a spotlight so bright nothing else was visible, a beautiful man in dark clothes, boots, and a Stetson was smiling right at Ian as he sang.

"Where would I be without the love of my man?" he sang.

Me. I'm his man.

"Yes, you are," the singer said, interrupting his song. "And I will always find you."

Billy. Of course, it's Billy. But as Ian started to walk toward him, a man's leering face appeared in the light behind Billy's right shoulder. He grabbed Billy around the neck and began to drag him out of the spotlight.

"You took what was mine," the man yelled. "Now you've gotta pay."

"Wait," Ian cried. "No. Billy!"

Billy didn't struggle. He kept sad eyes trained on Ian until he disappeared from sight.

IAN WAS on the edge of reality. *Oh God! My head!* The pain was excruciating. He heard something or someone moving around and then darkness consumed him again.

IAN WAS in his townhouse, filled with despair. He'd driven Billy away, and all he wanted was to be left alone to drown in his own

140

self-pity. But someone was banging on the door, over and over again. *Bang! Bang! Bang!*

Oh God, my head.

"This better be important," Ian muttered as he opened the door, ready to snarl angrily at the noisy intruder.

His emotion quickly changed from anger to shock and then just as quickly to rage. He recognized this visitor. All the hurt Ian had buried eight years ago instantly rushed to the surface, as fresh and fervent as it had been the day he'd left South Carolina forever.

Todd. His first lover. His betrayer.

"What the hell are you doing here?" he hissed.

Todd started to speak, but Ian tensed and almost involuntarily clenched his hand into a tight fist. He raised his arm to strike the unwanted intruder from his past.

Todd put his arms in front of his face. "Ian, don't!" he yelled. "Billy sent me! Hear me out, Ian, and then if you still want to beat me senseless, we'll give it a go."

Ian stared into Todd's eyes, unsure what to do next. Beat the man to a pulp? Listen to what he had to say and *then* beat the hell out of him? Overcome with exhaustion, Ian relaxed his fists, dropped his arm, and stepped aside as Todd Slocum entered his home.

"Say what you have to say and get out," he said as he closed the door behind them. "And what the hell does Billy have to do with this?"

"He asked me to come," Todd said. "He loves you."

He loves me. He loves me. He loves me.

"Yeah, well," Ian said, pinching the bridge of his nose against the brutal headache that made it hard to think. "After what you did to me eight years ago, I can't love anyone ever again, so you can thank yourself for whatever I've become."

"Ian, my parents played us both," Todd whispered.

"What are you talking about?" Ian barked back.

"Ian, they told me you said you never cared for me and accepted twenty thousand dollars to get out of town, and now because of Billy, I know they told you I accused you of rape. Ian," Todd said with tears in his eyes, "they played us, man, both of us. I

141

loved you, Ian. I could have never accused you of rape, but they spent hours convincing me that you sold me out for twenty grand, and after all, you did leave town."

Chilled to the bone, head pounding, Ian stood there, not sure he was hearing correctly. He finally muttered, "Yeah, I left town. I had to. They told me if I didn't, they would have me arrested for rape and that you were prepared to testify against me."

Todd moved to Ian's side and took his hand. "I know, man, I know. They lied to both of us." His words had a weird echo to them, like they were coming from a great distance down a long metal tunnel.

Ian reached for Todd to embrace him. He wanted to tell Todd he had loved him and would never have left him for any amount of money. But before he could touch him, Todd was drifting away from him. Fading from Ian's sight into a growing darkness.

IAN'S MIND was reeling. He slowly came back to the land of the living after taking so many blows to the head.

His head was pounding like someone was using a jackhammer on it, but he needed to get past that, clear the fog from his brain, and think. He didn't dare move, not wanting to alert Buck that he was awake, but he could feel Buck's eyes on him and that weirded him out. *Nothing you can do about that.*

Ian knew Billy would be here soon, whether Ian liked it or not. He tried to think about anything he could do to prepare for his arrival, but with few options, he quietly went to work on the ropes that bound his hands. Anything to keep him busy while giving him hope and distracting his mind from the obvious.

He hesitantly moved his wrists a little one way, then the other, trying to loosen his bindings. Billy would need him, and if he was hogtied like a calf at a rodeo, there was no way he could be of any help. But if he could eventually free his hands, he might be able to rip the duct tape and reach his ankles. It would take him a few minutes, but it was all the hope he had.

Ian listened carefully as the sounds of bourbon sloshing around and Buck swallowing echoed off the walls of the small enclosure each time Buck put the bottle to his lips. With each sip, Ian's—and Billy's!—chances of survival increased. The drunker Buck became, the more mistakes he would make and the easier it would be to overpower him.

Jesus! I need to pee really badly. But he'd be damned if he was gonna give Buck the satisfaction of seeing him pee on himself while he was naked and secured to a table. In an attempt to not think about it, he allowed himself for the first time to think about what might happen when Billy got there. And he knew Billy. He *would* get there.

Ian went over the weapons situation. He knew Buck had the large pocketknife, but he hadn't seen a gun. *That doesn't mean there isn't one*, he cautioned himself. But, knowing Buck, he would have been waving it around trying to intimidate Ian if he actually had one. He remembered seeing Buck stack a couple of pipes in the corner of the room, and that had alarmed him—hitting someone over the head seemed to be Buck's modus operandi.

Ian gave some thought to where he was being held. As far as his limited view of the room allowed, there seemed to be only one way in and one way out. But he had no idea where he was. Was he in a room inside another building? Ian couldn't really see the door, but every time Buck left the enclosure, there was a clanking sound like something locking. He'd heard the sound before but couldn't quite put his finger on it. Was it daylight beyond the door? No, it couldn't be, as each time Buck opened and closed the door, no noticeable light entered the room.

Am I doomed? Is Billy doomed? It can't end like this. I won't let it.

God! I need to pee!

No! Ian, focus!

Ian's thoughts were interrupted by the sound of duct tape tearing. He didn't dare open his eyes for fear of Buck's retaliation, and he remained still as Buck covered his mouth with the tape.

"That should keep you quiet," Buck said.

Shit! No way Ian could warn Billy when he arrived. But… *Buck is slurring his words worse than before.* That was cause for hope, wasn't it?

BUCK WENT back to his seat and looked at his watch. *Five fifty-five.*

He picked up his prepaid phone, slid the battery back in place, and hit the redial button.

Billy answered immediately.

"Buck?" Billy asked. "Where are you?"

"All in good time," Buck answered. "Do you have the money?"

"Yes," Billy replied. "A half million dollars."

"In small bills?"

"Yes, damn it," Billy said with an annoyed tone in his voice.

"Don't get testy with me, you little faggot. Unless… you never want to see your boyfriend again."

"Just tell me where you are," Billy pleaded.

"And the cops?"

"I ditched them," Billy confessed. "I took the money and ditched the tracking device. They have no idea where I am."

"Good queer," Buck said tauntingly. "Now, where are you?"

"I'm in the Lower 9th Ward," Billy confessed.

Buck panicked for a quick second. *He's so close. How in the fuck did they know where I am?*

Think, Buck!

He stood again, and this time the room spun a little. "Fuck," he said, gripping the small table next to his chair.

They may be close, but they have no idea where you are or they would have stormed the place already. Calm down and don't fuck this up.

"Buck?" Billy said. "Are you there?"

"Listen carefully, homo, 'cause I'll only say this once."

"I'm listening."

"I'm in an abandoned building at the Alfred Lawless High School," Buck said, giving Billy explicit directions. "Once you are parked in the loading bin with the door closed behind you, enter the cafeteria, walk to the right behind the service area, and straight ahead you'll find the walk-in refrigerator. Drop the bag of money on the table outside of the refrigerator and then lock yourself inside. That's where you'll find your boyfriend."

Buck disconnected the call. He didn't have much time. He hadn't realized Eagan would be so close. He attempted to drag a small table toward the door, but as he took a step, he stumbled and fell against the wall. He barely caught himself before he went down. He steadied himself and tried again. This time he managed to drag the table through the door and slid it into position outside the refrigerator. He went back in, closing the door behind him, and retrieved the pipes and placed them at the left side of the door in the corner. With nothing else to do but wait, he focused his attention on Ian.

He again brushed Ian's blond hair out of his eyes and stroked it softly. "Your boyfriend will be here shortly," he whispered. "And when he gets here, I'm gonna have a little fun with the both of you."

His captive didn't move, so Buck assumed he was still out like a light. He ran his fingers down Ian's back and then farther to the crack of Ian's ass. He circled Ian's opening and began to almost salivate. "Just a little longer," Buck whispered. "And then I'm gonna show you what it feels like to have a real man fuck you."

BILLY WAS at the abandoned high school in less than ten minutes. He located the building and fought with the first loading-bin door, but it wouldn't open. He tried the next, and when it opened, saw a beat-up pickup truck that must've belonged to Buck occupying that space. He cursed under his breath and went to the third door. With a little effort, he was able to get it open. He drove inside, threw the truck into park, closed the garage door behind him, and bolted for the interior entrance. With the bag of money tightly secured in his left hand, he reached behind him with his right and retrieved his dad's .45 from his belt, pulled back the hammer, and cocked it.

145

Since Buck had instructed him to leave the money outside the refrigerator and then lock himself inside, he figured Buck would be watching his movements from a safe distance. He approached cautiously and peered into the long, narrow, wire-reinforced vertical window in the door. He didn't see Buck, but he hadn't really expected to. He turned the doorknob and entered the building slowly. He saw the service area across the room and guardedly worked his way to it, staying down and keeping a diligent eye out for Buck, half expecting the same sort of ambush Buck had bestowed on Billy at the Lazy H Ranch five years ago.

When he spotted the small table outside the large refrigerator door, he sighed a breath of relief. *Ian's right behind that door. Hold on, Ian, I'm almost there.*

Billy crouched down farther, held his gun out in of front of him, and turned around and around as he moved across the large prep room, keeping a three-hundred-and-sixty-degree view. He reached the refrigerator without incident, placed the bag on the table as instructed, and put his hand on the door latch. He hesitated before opening it. What if it was booby-trapped with some sort of explosives? On second thought, though, however stupid Buck was, he wasn't stupid enough to risk having the money blown to pieces.

Billy pulled the door open slowly and saw the silhouette of Ian's still, naked body tied to a table at the far end of the refrigerator.

"Ian!" Billy screamed, unable to stop himself from running toward the table. Halfway there, he was stopped in his tracks by a solid blow to his left shoulder. The force of the blow caused his gun to fly out of his hand. Billy watched the gun sail through the air and hit the floor, the impact causing it to go off, the kick sending it across the floor to the opposite side of the room. A loud noise echoed through the small enclosure and Billy ducked and grabbed his ears to lessen the deafening sound. Luckily the stray bullet embedded itself in the metal wall of the refrigerator rather than ricocheting off to potentially hit one of them. Although Billy wouldn't have minded at all if it had hit Buck.

When Billy stood upright again, he saw Buck out of the corner of his left eye, standing there and poised to swing again. He threw

146

his hands up, blocked the blow, and caught the pipe midswing. Billy yanked the pipe out of Buck's hands and wound up to attempt a swing of his own, but before he could get the pipe far enough back to make a solid impact, Buck had spun around and grabbed another pipe, and this time Billy took the blow to the side of his head. The blow reverberated throughout his entire body, sending vibrations all the way to his core. The room began to spin, and then everything faded to black.

Chapter Ten

IT HADN'T taken the NOPD or Beau and Tollison long to realize what Billy was up to. When Billy had said he was taking a drive, Beau had given Hebert a knowing glance. When he hadn't come back in time for Buck's six o'clock call, they realized their suspicions had been right. But luckily they were prepared and jumped into action.

Tollison physically traced Billy's whereabouts using the tracking device they had put on him, but minutes later he found the device in one of the abandoned houses they'd searched earlier. Meanwhile Hebert got confirmation that the six o'clock call had indeed come in to Billy's phone, and they were able to determine both phones were using the same cell tower.

While Beau got to work tracking Billy's cell phone, Hebert was told Buck hadn't disabled his phone after the last call, and they'd been able to pinpoint his exact location. When Beau tracked down Billy's location, they knew they had them both. Their only hope was that Ian was there as well and they weren't too late.

IAN LOOKED on in horror, unable to do anything to protect Billy. His eyes scanned the room frantically as his own silent screams filled his head. He'd seen the entire episode unfold in front of his eyes. The first blow to Billy's shoulder, the gun flying through the air then exploding on impact, the second blow striking Billy in the head, and then Billy's lifeless body dropping to the floor.

In a sense Ian likened the entire experience to one of those stories you heard about someone going in for surgery and being put to sleep, but they were not really sleeping. They could feel every incision, see everything as it happened but were sadly powerless to move or make a sound to stop any of it. People described the pain as gut wrenching and unbearable, and at this moment, Ian could totally relate.

Feelings of gloom and despair again consumed Ian as he watched Buck hoist Billy's body off the floor and position him faceup on the table Buck had set next to his own. Seeing Billy's limp body lying on the table made Ian frantically try again to get his hands free. He imagined cutting his hands off at the wrists so he could slip out of his bindings and run to Billy. But it was a fantasy. His hands were still secure, as were his feet. It appeared Buck had plans for both of them, and neither was going to get out alive.

Ian studied Billy's handsome face. The bright red blood stood out harshly against his jet-black hair as it ran down Billy's chiseled cheek. Ian had no idea how badly Billy was hurt and wanted so desperately to be able to touch him, any part of him.

Ian watched in horror as Buck pulled Billy's boots and socks off. He paused and gently rubbed Billy's bare feet.

"Does that feel good, Eagan?" he asked. "I sure hope it does 'cause everything is about to take a turn for the worse, and I don't think it's gonna feel so good then."

Buck continued to caress Billy's feet. "What's that you say? What do I mean?" Buck asked Billy's motionless body, his words slightly slurring. "Well I'm glad you asked. See, faggot, after a long wait, I'm about to even up the score big time. Yes. That's right. You took things from me, and I'm about to take everything from you. A little bit at a time," he added, looking over at Ian and smiling an ugly smile.

Buck suddenly stopped stroking Billy's feet, and Ian's eyes widened as Buck's gaze moved up Billy's pant legs to his crotch to eye the bulge there. Buck moved up the table, unbuckled Billy's belt and jeans, and slid them down to his ankles and off.

What the fuck? Ian thought as Buck took out his pocketknife and slid it under Billy's T-shirt at his abdomen. He ran the blade all the way up to Billy's neck, slicing the shirt in two. The shirt separated, exposing Billy's bare chest. Ian watched as Buck stared at

Billy almost longingly. He cut away the sleeves, and the shirt fell away, exposing Billy's biceps.

Buck ran the blade around both of Billy's nipples and then down Billy's chest to his belly button, moving the tip around in the little patch of hair above the waistband of Billy's underwear. Ian's eyes widened again when, in one quick motion, Buck sliced Billy's underwear once down each leg and ripped it out from underneath him. Billy was now totally naked and exposed as Buck gazed motionless at his limp body.

Suddenly Buck shook his head as if fighting some internal force. Ian watched silently as Buck secured Billy's arms and legs to the table as he had done with Ian's and then taped Billy's midsection in much the same way. But he wasn't stopping there. Buck then secured Billy's head to the table facing Ian and then went one step further and duct-taped Billy's eyelids open.

"Sorry Eagan," Buck said. "But no closing your eyes or turning your head away during this show."

Ian's eyes followed Buck out of the refrigerator. When he returned, he was carrying a brown bag. He gathered up Billy's gun and laid it next to the bag, along with his pocketknife and phone.

BILLY DRIFTED between consciousness and darkness. He felt himself being maneuvered, but then felt sure he was only imagining someone rubbing his feet. He tried to open his eyes, but although his mind was willing, his body wasn't cooperating. He was suddenly cold and imagined a shiver going up and down his spine. Then a foggy vision of Ian appeared in his mind. At first glance Ian had tape over his mouth. But on a closer look, he was also naked and tied to a table. Ian's bright green eyes were calling to him, but Billy still couldn't move.

Then, almost instantly, Billy remembered where he was and what was happening to them. That image of Ian wasn't something in his mind. It was the real thing. He was looking at Ian, bound, naked, and gagged. Billy tried to blink to clear his sight, but his eyes weren't working. When he tried to move his head and the rest of his body, he

150

quickly realized he, too, was secured to something. And based on the chill that enveloped his body, he was also naked. In a panic, Billy tried to call out for help, but his mouth was bound, as was Ian's.

"No, Buck! Wait! Stop!" Billy yelled into the tape as he met Buck's eyes. He suddenly knew what Buck was planning, and he couldn't allow it to happen.

Buck was standing at Ian's feet with his pants down to his knees. As Billy watched, Buck spit into his hand and rubbed his saliva around Ian's opening as he stroked his almost rock-hard cock, preparing himself.

Billy frantically struggled to free himself, but nothing gave way. Buck was eyeing him with a sadistic smile as he slid his hand up and down his shaft. Buck took a couple of steps in Billy's direction and slapped him in the face with his cock.

"This is what your boyfriend is about to get up his man pussy." Buck stepped to the side and ran his finger down the crack of Billy's ass, circling his opening. "Don't worry," he said. "You're gonna get some of this too."

Buck walked over, grabbed the .45, and headed back toward Ian.

If I can just keep him away from Ian!

"Take me," Billy yelled against the tape as loudly as he could.

Buck stopped, looked at him, and gave him a sinister smile. "Not a chance. But you're up next."

Billy cast a pleading glance in Buck's direction that he hoped conveyed his thoughts. But no such luck. Buck saw right through that and smiled again.

"I'm not fooled by your attempts to keep me away from your boyfriend. He goes first and then you." He held up the gun and waved it around. "And... then when I'm satisfied, you both die."

Billy watched in horror as Buck laid the gun down at Ian's head, climbed onto the table, and stretched out on top of Ian, his cock positioned against Ian's opening.

No! God, no. Don't let him do this!

Buck sighed and was about to force himself inside when the door to the refrigerator swung open so forcefully it banged against the wall with a metallic *clang*.

151

"Freeze," Detective Hebert yelled. Beau was right behind him, both their guns drawn.

Billy moaned to alert Hebert to Buck's gun, but before he could do anything else, Buck grabbed the gun, held it close to his chest, and came up onto his knees. He quickly raised his left hand in surrender and then whipped around, aiming the gun at Hebert.

Apparently both men had seen the gun and were prepared for Buck's actions. Before Buck could fire, Hebert fired one single shot. Buck stiffened, arched his back, slowly fell forward, and collapsed on top of Ian. His pants were still at his knees.

Hebert approached Ian and Buck cautiously. "Shots fired," he called into his shoulder radio. "Request medical assistance."

When Buck didn't move, Hebert shoved Buck off of Ian, and he rolled to the floor with a thud.

BILLY WATCHED as Hebert worked diligently to free Ian. Beau did the same for him. Beau first freed Billy's head and then carefully removed the tape from his eyelids. Billy felt him working on the bindings around his feet and then cutting into the duct tape securing his torso. His heart was racing, and he desperately needed to be free. Although he could see Ian on the table next to him, he wouldn't be certain he was all right until he had him in his arms. Billy used every bit of strength he could dredge up and lifted his torso off the table, ripping through what was left of the duct tape. He slid off the table. Beau was still working on his hands, but he dragged the table behind him to get to Ian.

Ian sat up just as Beau released Billy's hands, and Billy ran the last few feet to Ian. He stopped and stood in front of Ian, his entire body beginning to tremble. Billy's muscles ignored his will to move until Ian reached out and touched his arm gently. Then he launched himself into Ian's arms and buried his face in Ian's neck. With Ian safe and the adrenaline still flowing rapidly through Billy's veins, relief overtook him and he began to cry, softly at first, then the sobs followed.

Ian soothed him by gently rubbing his back and telling him it was all going to be okay. *Everything* was going to okay.

Billy turned frantically and threw himself in front of Ian in a protective stance when Tollison, John, Jules, and Josh burst into the room. They stopped short when they saw Billy and Ian together, and Billy relaxed as well but turned right back to Ian.

"Are you all right? Did he…?"

Ian shook his head from side to side. "No, he didn't, and I'm okay. Still a little groggy from the drugs, but I'm okay." He reached up and touched the dried blood on Billy's head. "What about you?"

Billy took Ian's hand and brought it to his lips and gently kissed it. "Just a bump on the head."

Then reality hit him hard. "Oh God, Ian, I thought I'd lost you forever."

"I know," Ian agreed. "But somehow I knew you would come."

"No matter what happens, I'll always find you," Billy said. "Always."

He wrapped Ian in his arms. "I love you, Ian."

"I love you too, Cowboy. God, do I need to pee."

Epilogue

IAN AND Billy stood hand in hand, admiring how far along the remodeling of their new French Quarter townhouse had come. The walls were studded, the plumbing and electrical roughed in, and the hardwood was down on all three floors.

The ground floor consisted of an entry foyer, a small kitchenette to serve the pool, and a patio area, along with three guest bedrooms and three en suite bathrooms. The entire second floor was a gourmet kitchen, great room, and powder room, and the third floor was their master suite, consisting of their bedroom, bathroom, a workout room, and Ian's office.

Billy's tour was scheduled to kick off in one week, leaving a shitload of things for him to do and not much time to do them. Billy tried to drag Ian upstairs with him and the architect to review the updated plans once more before they left, but Ian needed to deal with a few demons of his own right where he was. In the few times they'd been back to the townhouse since the abduction, mostly to finalize the plans, they'd come in together, never left each other's side, and then headed right back out. But this time Ian wanted to tackle his memories head on and once and for all. If he was going to live here at some point, he had to face whatever it was that was bothering him so he could feel safe and secure in their new home.

Ian tried to release Billy's hand, but Billy held fast. "Go on up. I'll join you in a minute," Ian assured him.

Billy, probably sensing what Ian needed to do, offered him a weak smile and reluctantly released his hand. He headed up the stairs, looking back every few steps, undoubtedly to make sure Ian was still there and all right. Ian smiled to reassure Billy all was okay until he finally disappeared at the top of the stairs. He and Billy had never been so tuned in to each other's fears and emotions as they had been since the abduction, and that had secured their bond even more, if that was possible. The thought that he could love and trust someone so completely sometimes floored Ian.

Ian stood in front of the french doors looking out onto Royal Street and ran his hand absentmindedly along the doorsill. The memory hit him hard, engaging all his senses as if it were happening all over again. He realized he was standing in the same location where Buck had found him some seven weeks ago. Ian thought about their entire ordeal, and it seemed at one and the same time like a distant but oh so immediate nightmare.

WHEN THE EMTs had arrived, Buck had no vital signs, and they'd quickly called in a coroner to pronounce him dead on the scene. Ian had tried at the time, but he couldn't find any sympathy for the guy. Now it seemed a little easier because over time he'd realized Buck had gotten the short end of the stick when it came to his family—or lack thereof. But he also kept reminding himself many other people had gone through some of the same things Buck had dealt with but had not turned into what Buck had become.

Ian also reminded himself that things always happen for a reason, and if Buck had survived, he and Billy would be forever looking over their shoulder, studying every shadow and waiting for the next attack.

"No! This is better," he whispered.

In that small walk-in refrigerator in an abandoned school in the Lower 9th Ward of New Orleans, Billy, in his own stubborn way, had insisted the EMTs examine Ian first. And only after Ian had been pronounced in no immediate danger did he allow the EMTs to examine him. Detective Hebert had given them both their pants and shirts, and they had climbed side by side, hand in hand, onto the same table that earlier had been Ian's prison.

Ian watched as they'd cleaned Billy's head and added a few stitches to secure the wound. They were both loaded into the emergency response unit and taken to the hospital, where they were admitted, had brain scans done, and were kept overnight for observation. The doctor wanted to keep them longer, but Ian wasn't surprised when Billy balked at the idea, and Ian had no intention of staying there a minute longer without him.

The ride back to the North Shore the next day seemed to take a year instead of an hour. And to top it off, when they arrived, they were greeted by a barrage of news trucks with satellite dishes raised high into the sky and officers of the law trying to keep order.

Later they found out that Jean had handled the press by making a short statement that Billy and Ian were both okay, asking for privacy, and leaving it at that.

The news coverage that followed had been hugely positive. Of course there had been the same small percentage of naysayers touting that Billy and Ian had gotten their due and paid penance for their homosexual sins, but by and large they'd been supported in every way. In the days that followed, they'd received calls, cards, and letters with tons of well wishes from their country music family. And in fact, ticket sales for Billy's concert were up enough to add second shows to many of the scheduled cities and even add a few more cities to the mix.

BACK IN the present, Ian gazed at the tourists strolling aimlessly along Royal Street below, many of them never knowing what might await them around the next bend. The sad thing was, now Ian and Billy did know, and it was something they could never *un*know.

Ian turned and looked at the stairs he'd tried to escape down when Buck had tackled him. A chill ran through him and his stomach lurched when he remembered the stick of the needle as it had been jabbed into his neck. And then waking up naked and tied to a table, after Buck had done God knows what to him. He would never share that part with Billy. There was no need. It would only hurt Billy more, and besides, it wouldn't change anything. But he'd sensed Buck had done something to him and was just as glad he would never really know for sure.

How blessed Ian felt to have a man like Billy to love, and to have Billy love him so completely in return and vow to always protect him. It wasn't so long ago they'd almost lost it all. Once because of Ian's own fears and emotional insecurities, but that time Billy had saved him from himself and eventually won him over. The second time was at the hands of Buck Stevens, but Ian had been lucky enough to save Billy that time. Now, recently, Buck Stevens had threatened them again. But Billy had come for him and saved him, with a little help from their friends, family, and some smart and dedicated cops and PIs. If nothing else these experiences had made Ian realize how fragile the cycle of life is and how, in a flash, it can be totally turned upside down. They had dodged three bullets and survived. How many more chances would they get?

In that short amount of time, Ian decided the only way he would be able to move forward was to face life head on, on his own terms. Billy had proven himself over and over, and Ian was secure in that fact. Billy would never allow anything to come between them, and Ian felt the same. No more looking over his shoulder. No more wondering what was ahead for them. He would take it as it came with no regrets and no looking back.

Ian turned when he heard Billy and the architect coming down the stairs. Ian and Billy said their good-byes with a promise to stay in touch and receive regular updates on the progress. Billy walked the man out and was immediately back at Ian's side, his arm draped over Ian's shoulder. "You okay?"

"I'm better than okay," Ian said. "Tomorrow we start another new chapter of our life."

"Are you gonna feel safe here when we move in?" Billy asked.

Ian smiled. He'd never shared his doubts and fears about living here with Billy, but as usual, he hadn't had to. Billy was right there in tune with his every thought.

"I think I am," Ian said, kissing Billy on the cheek. "Especially if you're here with me."

"Always," Billy replied, wrapping Ian in his arms.

"How about you?" Ian asked, wondering if Billy had any doubts of his own.

"Ian," Billy said, pulling back and gazing into Ian's eyes. "*You* are my safe haven. Regardless of where we are, I'm always safe when I'm in your arms."

Billy dropped down to one knee. His bright blue eyes were looking up at Ian and sparkling. The sight made Ian's heart beat so rapidly he thought it might beat right out of his chest.

Billy dug into his pocket, retrieved a little black velvet box, opened it, and showed it to Ian. "Ian Dillon. I love you with all my heart. Will you marry me?"

Ian dropped down to his knees, threw his arms around Billy, and glanced up to the heavens. "Yes!" he shouted at the top of his lungs. Ian looked Billy in the eyes. "I love you with all my heart!"

SEVENTY THOUSAND people were on their feet at the New Orleans Mercedes Benz Superdome chanting "Billy! Billy! Billy!" and stomping and yelling for more as Billy finished his second encore. He removed the microphone from its stand, and as he spoke, he walked to the side of the stage where Ian was standing.

"I can't thank you all enough for the love and support you've shown me tonight and in the last five years." Ian's eyes widened as he approached. Billy smiled, took Ian by the hand, and led him out to center stage.

"You all remember Ian Dillon, my manager and life partner," he said. The crowd erupted into applause.

"In addition to the love and support you've shown me over the years, your acceptance of Ian in my life is remarkable. You've never wavered in your loyalty, and for that we will always be grateful. But tonight—" Billy paused until the crowd settled down. "—tonight I have a surprise for you and for Ian."

Billy looked at Ian, who was staring at him curiously, wearing a crooked grin. One of the stagehands came out and handed Ian a microphone.

Ian looked out into the crowd. "I have no idea what's coming next, but I hope I don't have to apologize afterward."

The crowd came to life again, shouting, "Now! Now! Now!"

"Okay, okay!" Billy said. "Hold your horses."

Billy squeezed Ian's hand, and Ian smiled back at him. "You all remember my first number-one hit?" Billy asked as the crowd screamed again.

"I'm sure everyone remembers because I talked about it so much when the song first came out. But anyway, the song was written about my parents and the love they shared." Billy nodded at the front row. "And they're sitting right there, by the way. Mom and Dad, stand up and wave to the nice people."

Billy's parents stood up, turned around, and waved like crazy. Billy smiled and looked at Ian when their faces appeared on the JumboTron. "In fact, all of you down there in the first row stand up and take a bow. These people are my family and friends. If it weren't for them, Ian and I might not be here right now."

Billy watched as his entire family, as well as Jean and Jules, Josh and Suzie, Beau and Tollison, Auggie Hebert and his wife, Bruce Jenkins and his boyfriend, and last but not least, Officer Boudreaux and his partner Roy all stood up and took various bows, grinned at themselves on the JumboTron, and waved at the crowds.

"Okay! That's enough, you hams!" Billy teased. "This is my concert. Sit back down."

"Now where was I? Oh yeah, the song. So Mom and Dad, I did this out of love, and I hope you're not upset, but I rewrote the lyrics... for Ian."

Again the crowd stomped and chanted. But instead of chanting "Billy," this time they chanted, "Ian! Ian! Ian!"

Billy glanced over at Ian, who was smiling from ear to ear with a surprised look painted all over his face. "For me?" he asked, looking back and forth between Billy and the audience.

"Just for you!" Billy said. "And—" He paused as he waited for the audience to settle down again. "—on a more serious note."

Billy's voice took on a somber tone, and the audience remained silent. "If you watch the news or read the tabloids, you already know Ian and I have been through a lot in the last few months, so I wanted to do something to show Ian and the world how much I love him."

After a moment of silence, Billy smiled widely at the crowd, and they took the opportunity to burst into thunderous applause once more.

"Now," Billy said, "this is the first time I've ever sang the song in public and probably the last, but since New Orleans is my hometown and soon to be a refuge for Ian and I when we're not on tour, I wanted y'all to be part of this."

Billy led Ian to the edge of the stage in front of his family and friends, tugged Ian down with him as he sat, and let his legs dangle off the edge of the stage. The lights dimmed, and a single spotlight encompassed Billy and Ian, their faces alone appearing on the JumboTron. Billy nodded to the band and the intro started. He looked at Ian and began to sing.

Our road to love had its bumpy beginnings, and sometimes we lost our footing,
But we traveled it well, each bump and each swell, thank heavens you were so willing.
You gave me a chance to prove who I am, to prove that I was worthy.
Somehow, some way, you let me in, and my life is now so fulfilling.

Where would I be without the love of a man?
You make me smile and all the while, keep me safe in your embrace.

*My life would be so empty and cold, if I didn't
have you to hold.*
You are everything that I am and forever will be.

*Through life's ups and downs and the fame
that we found,*
You held our lives together.
You support me still as I know you always will,
*And with that, there's no storm we cannot
weather*

Not everyone gets the strength of our love.
In the end it makes no difference.
With you by my side, my love I won't hide
As we journey through our existence.

Where would I be without the love of my man?
*You make me smile and all the while, keep me
safe in your embrace.*
*My life would be so empty and cold, if I didn't
have you to hold.*
You are everything that I am and forever will be.

*We're here and we're strong, living life on
our own.*
As long as we're together, no one can destroy me.
*You're my love for all time, both now and
beyond,*
And I'll love you for eternity

Where would I be without the love of my man?
*You make me smile and all the while, keep me
safe in your embrace.*
*My life would be so empty and cold, if I didn't
have you to hold.*
You are everything that I am and forever will be.

As Billy sang the last chorus, he stood and pulled Ian up with him. The entire audience had small flashlights and cigarette lighters and cell phones held high in the air, waving them back and forth in time with the music.

After Billy sang the final note, he took a bow. He wrapped Ian in his arms, released him, and then raised their joined hands over their heads. "Good night, everyone, and from the bottom of our hearts, we thank you and we love you. Good night!"

Keeping reading for

Tires flying over the interstate, college student Ian Dillon can't get out of Greenville, SC quickly enough. As he watches his entire life fading away in his rearview mirror, his thoughts are only of his lover, Todd, and the memories of their time together, now completely shattered by Todd's incomprehensible betrayal. His mind still reeling, Ian drives through the night until a split second decision guides him to Nashville, Tennessee. Everything will be better there. It has to be!

http://www.dreamspinnerpress.com

IAN DILLON drove like a bat out of hell through the foggy and rainy South Carolina night, heading for the quickest route out of Greenville. As he barreled down Interstate 385, he kept his fingers wrapped tightly around the steering wheel as if it were the last thing he had to actually hold on to. He pulled onto the entrance ramp to Interstate 85 not caring if he was going north or south, just knowing he needed to get as far away as possible from the memories that were assaulting him, threatening his very existence.

As he blinked back the welling up in his eyes, he watched Greenville disappear in his rearview mirror and wondered how he was ever going to erase the last two years of his life. He was just twenty years old, but so many emotions were flooding his mind—anger, love, resentment, but most of all, betrayal. He suddenly realized that from this point forward, the pain he was feeling would forever be associated with being in love. He vowed right then and there never to expose himself to the possibly of such despair again.

In an attempt to fight off an impending panic attack, Ian pulled into the passing lane, stomped the accelerator, and sped past a delivery truck. In his mind, the faster he drove, the faster he could get away from his bigoted parents and Todd Slocum, the man who had broken him so completely he would never feel whole or be the same again. As he barreled down the highway with no real destination in mind, he had no idea how he was ever going to get over the scorching pain caused by the man who had vowed to protect and love him forever. So he just drove on.

DING. IAN recognized the simple sound and slowly came out of his emotional fog. He glanced at the fuel gauge; it was quickly approaching the empty mark. Dawn was breaking ahead, and the sun was just starting to peek above the pine-tree-lined highway to his right. *My God, I must have driven through the night, and I guess I'm going north.*

Ian shifted in his seat. He was very thirsty, but more importantly, he needed to pee. As he approached the next off-ramp, the green highway road sign ahead announced Interstate 40 West, Two Miles. He knew Interstate 40 led to Nashville and thought, *Why not.* Without hesitation Ian hit the gas pedal and headed to Tennessee.

After merging onto I-40, he took the first exit and stopped for gas. Once he had relieved himself, he filled his truck and bought an energy drink.

On the highway again, Ian downed the contents of the little black bottle and tossed the empty container onto the seat next to him. He knew he should be sleepy, but he wasn't. Exhausted, yes. Numb as hell, sure. But not sleepy.

With nothing but the hum of his truck's engine to distract him, he once again felt the ache in his heart. He started to feel clammy all over, and his palms began to sweat. Ian's stomach did a backflip, and he thought he might lose what little was in his gut, but he swallowed hard and did his best to keep it down and hold the heaves at bay.

Unfortunately, he wasn't as successful holding his thoughts at bay. His father's words replayed in his head. "Get out of here and never come back. You might be able to evade prison, but prison is nothing like the fires of hell, and one day that's where you'll surely end up."

Hurt, disappointment, and dread consumed him.

I can't keep reliving this over and over. Not again.

Ian struggled to get control of his emotions. He needed something to derail his thoughts, a distraction. He needed a plan. "But a plan for what?" a little voice in his head taunted. "You have a family that hates you, a lover who sold you out, half an education, and about eighteen hundred dollars to your name. What is all this going to get you?"

Nothing. Absolutely nothing.

Ian drove the rest of the morning on autopilot, maneuvering his truck by and large from habit rather than paying any attention to the road. He got lost in his thoughts while his broken heart ached unbearably. He continually tried to push his emotions from his mind, but they always wormed their way right back in again.

A sudden growl from his stomach broke his concentration and reminded him he hadn't eaten since yesterday morning. He hoped being hungry was a good sign. Maybe the doom that surrounded him was finally lifting, and maybe, just maybe, he could make a decision or two about where he was going and what he was going to do when he got there.

WHEN IAN saw the Nashville skyline, he decided it was time to stop. He exited I-40 and pulled into the first fast-food drive-through he came to. He ordered a burger and a Coke to go and continued on in searched of a place to stay. As he drove down the access road, he noticed a sign that said Nash's Motor Lodge, One Mile.

The motel parking lot was empty except for one eighteen-wheeler and an old, beat-up Chevy. It wasn't the nicest place he had ever stayed, but he figured he didn't deserve any better.

Ian stepped into a tiny lobby and took in the heavy scent of cigarette smoke combined with mold and mildew. He rang the dingy brass bell on what he supposed was the front desk. A few seconds later, a little man with a half-eaten sandwich in his hand, chewing vigorously, stepped in front of the thick, bulletproof Plexiglas window.

The man just looked at him, still munching away.

"Hi. I need a room, please."

The man glanced past Ian like he was looking for someone else and spoke with a mouth full. "How many hours?"

Ian looked behind him like maybe there *was* someone else in the room, but other than him, the little office was empty. "For one night," he replied.

The man turned to a board with keys hanging on it and chose one. "Thirty-nine dollars," he said with a strong accent.

After paying cash, Ian drove around to the back of the lodge and found room seventeen. He reached behind the seat, grabbed his gym bag, and silently thanked himself for being a gym junkie. In that bag was everything he had. It held his toiletries, a change of clothes, a pair of sneakers, and a few other incidentals. He'd been in such a state when he left that he hadn't taken anything with him except what he was wearing.

Sliding the key into the lock, Ian opened the door and was instantly hit with a damp, musty smell. The room felt heavy and very dark. Whether it was the room or his mood, he couldn't really tell. The carpet below his feet was worn and badly stained, but the space held a bed, a bathroom, and a television, way more than he needed. He sat on the end of the bed and ran his fingers through his hair. He rested his elbows on his knees and cradled his face in his hands. Taking a deep breath, Ian exhaled as a single tear slid down one cheek. He immediately lifted his head and willed himself not to cry. He wasn't ready to cry. The wounds were too fresh and deep, and if the tears started, the floodgates would open, and there was no telling what might happen next.

He looked down and saw the bag containing his burger sitting next to him on the bed. He removed the burger, peeled back the wrapper, and took a small bite, but quickly realized he didn't have the stomach for it and tossed it in the trash can.

Ian pulled off his boots, scooted up to the head of the bed, and propped two cheap foam pillows under his head. He stared up at the coffee colored water stains on the ceiling and listened intently to the drip of the bathroom faucet. *Drip. Drip. Drip.* The simple sound was almost deafening. He grabbed the remote from the bedside table and switched on the television. Anything to drown out the dripping sound. His eyelids became very heavy, but the second he closed his eyes, he saw the look on his parents' faces and heard their voices in his head.

"The Slocums said Todd told them you raped and blackmailed him?"

How could Todd have said that?

At that moment, he'd hated the man he'd so desperately loved. Now he suddenly felt an overwhelming sadness and longing for Todd deep in the pit of his stomach. The same man who had so hurtfully betrayed him and thrown him under the bus to save his own hide.

"My entire life is over. In the blink of an eye, I have nothing," Ian whispered to himself.

He couldn't hold back the tears any longer and finally allowed himself to cry. When he eventually stopped sobbing, his body gave in to mental and physical exhaustion, and he fell into a deep sleep.

CONFUSED AND disoriented, Ian awoke to the sound of Diane Sawyer reading the evening news. It took him a minute to remember where he was and what had happened, but the flood of emotions didn't take long to rush back in and drown his mind with total darkness.

He looked at the clock on the nightstand. *Six forty-five. I can't believe I slept all day.*

As Diane read the teleprompter, describing some crazy person who'd attempted to scale the fence of the White House and got taken out by the Secret Service, Ian decided he needed a shower and something to eat.

He walked into the bathroom, turned on the faucet, and removed his clothes, dropping them into a pile on the floor. He sat on the edge of the tub and again cradled his head in his hands, while he waited for the water to heat up. "Fuck! Fuck! Fuck!" he whispered, still wondering how he'd ended up in this godforsaken place.

Ian took a quick lukewarm shower, dressed, and left in search of somewhere to get a bite to eat. After driving around for thirty minutes or so, he settled on Millie's Pub, which was on the corner of Broadway and Second Avenue. The diner-like restaurant was well into the dinner rush, but there was one seat available at the counter. *How ironic*, he thought. *In just twenty-four hours my life has become a seat for one.*

The waitress came over and greeted him with a warm smile. Fern, as her name tag indicated, gave him a menu and told him about the specials. He settled on meat loaf, mashed potatoes, and a glass of milk.

When Fern placed his dinner on the counter, he ate more out of necessity than desire. After he was through nibbling at what was left of his dinner, he paid the check, left Fern a generous tip, and walked back to his truck.

Once again seated in his truck, he was suddenly overtaken with emotion. He folded his arms on the steering wheel and laid his head down. The events of late were coming at him again, strong and hard. Another tear escaped his eye and ran down his cheek. He wiped it away with the back of his hand and cursed himself for giving in to his emotions. He still had to decide where to go and what to do, but his mind and heart were so full, he was having a hard time sorting through it all.

Staying in Nashville was certainly an option, so he decided to give it a couple of days and see if an opportunity might present itself. If nothing happened for him here, he would move on. Where, he didn't know, but at least in a couple of days he would hopefully be thinking a little clearer and could come up with another game plan.

With that settled he lifted his head and tried to get his bearings. Nightclubs, restaurants, and lounges lined Broadway on both sides. The street was busy with traffic, coming and going. People were strolling hand in hand on both sides of the streets, reading menus on the sidewalk and just having a simple evening.

Out the corner of his eye, he noticed a flashing neon sign in the next block with a large figure that seemed to be a flower of some sort. As he strained he could barely make out the writing. Jean's Magnolia Saloon.

It took him about two minutes to decide he could use a beer and a distraction. He got out of his truck, crossed the street, and walked down the block. When he opened the front door, he was assaulted with the smell of alcohol, sawdust, and smoke, and the sound of Tim McGraw's voice.

The lounge was much larger than it looked from the street. On one side a large mahogany bar ran the full length of the room, and opposite the bar was a raised stage with a colorful set of drums, an electric keyboard, and various musical instruments on stands. In the center of the room was an expansive oblong dance floor, surrounded by split rail fencing with openings at each end and what looked and smelled like fresh sawdust scattered on the floor. Overstuffed chairs in numerous groupings, along with high cocktail tables and bar stools, completed the furnishings.

It was still pretty early, but there were quite a few patrons enjoying cocktails. Ian eyed the last seat at the far end of the bar, tucked away in the corner, and headed that way.

A tall, thin woman who looked to be in her early sixties walked over and placed a cocktail napkin in front of him. Her smile was warm and beaming, and coupled with her dark brown hair and deep brown eyes, she portrayed the epitome of kindness, strength, and sincerity. "What can I get for you, sweetie?"

"I don't think you have what I need behind that bar," Ian said, "so I'll just take a Bud Light."

The woman laid her hand on top of Ian's. "Sweetie, you'd be surprised at what I keep behind here."

This time Ian matched her smile.

"I don't recognize you. Have you been here before?"

"No, ma'am, I just got to town."

The woman leaned over the bar and whispered, "In my line of work, you become pretty good at reading faces. And… right now you look like you could use a friend."

She straightened again and stuck her hand out. "I'm Anna Jean James, but everyone calls me Jean. I own this establishment."

Ian accepted her hand. It was warm, and her grip was strong. "Ian Dillon, pleased to meet you, ma'am."

"Very pleased to meet you, Mr. Dillon," she said in a soft, caring voice.

"Ian, please."

"Okay. Ian it is," Jean said. "You know I don't usually bartend," she added. "But one of my boys left me high and dry, so I'm filling in tonight."

Someone walked up and took a seat at the bar a few seats down, and they both looked in that direction. "I'll be right back, honey," Jean said.

Ian watched her as she seemingly floated up and down the bar, greeting guests and refilling drinks, and he felt oddly comfortable with her.

While he waited for Jean to return, Ian thought about how many guys had probably sat at this very bar sharing their hard luck stories, and yet she still had the time to listen.

"Now back to you, honey," Jean said when she returned. "What brings you to Nashville and my saloon?"

Her voice and warm smile made him feel at ease and that she was genuinely interested in his story. *This must be what it feels like to have a mother you can go to with any problems, and she would understand.* A mother he no longer had. One, he realized, he'd never had.

Ian hesitated; then something made him start to speak. And once he did, he couldn't stop. He didn't know why, but he imagined it was the sheer need to talk to someone, anyone, who didn't know him and who hopefully wouldn't judge him.

He told her of betrayal by someone he truly loved and about being disowned and cast out by his own parents. But he was cautious, or so he thought, because he left out the fact that his love had been a man named Todd Slocum.

When he finished the story, Jean said "Honey, I don't think anyone should have to carry all this weight in a lifetime, not to mention a day."

She took his hand in hers and squeezed. "Ian, what was his name, honey, and how long had you two been together."

Shocked, Ian dropped his head and said Todd's name out loud for the first time in twenty-four hours. "Todd Slocum and two years," he responded with his head still hung. Jean put her hand under Ian's chin, lifted his head, and looked him in the eye.

"How did you know?" Ian asked.

"My son is gay and came out to my husband and me over twenty years ago. We've been around you sweet boys for twenty years, and the older I get, the better my gaydar gets."

"And you're okay with it?" Ian asked.

"Of course I am," Jean said. "I mean, why would I not be? A lot of people, especially in the South, still think this lifestyle is a choice. I don't believe that and never have. What sane person would choose a lifestyle that still comes with such grief? All because of the person you love. Personally, I can't see how a parent can turn away from their child, their flesh and blood, for any reason, but that's just me."

Ian eyed Jean with a weary look. "You know, you're probably the only link to my sanity right now."

Jean reached over and squeezed his hand again. "Have you decided where you're going from here, or what you're going to do?" she asked.

Ian shook his head from side to side. It was just too hard to think about.

"Look, honey," she said, "I have a small studio over the saloon. Nothing much to speak about, but it's clean, and I could use a little help around here. I can't pay a lot, but if you'll accept board as part of your salary, this could work out."

Ian thought about it for a moment. "I really appreciate that, but I know nothing about working in a bar. I think you'd be drawing the short straw."

"What's to know?" Jean asked. "You'll do a little of this and a little of that, whatever needs to be done, and before you know it, it'll be second nature to you."

"I don't know," Ian said.

"Oh come on," Jean pleaded. "I need someone, and you need a job. We'll start you off barbacking, then a little bartending and some bouncing at the door. You'll do fine."

Ian considered the proposal but didn't respond.

"You wouldn't know it by looking around now, but in about two hours, this place will be full to capacity," Jean said. "The Magnolia Saloon is quite the little career launcher. Most of the big talents you know today played here in the early years, and all the big talent scouts hang around hoping to find the next big thing."

Ian looked around and was very impressed with the entire place. But more so with Jean and the easy, nurturing way about her. He'd just spilled his guts to a complete stranger, who somehow didn't feel like a stranger at all. In fact, he felt as if he known her for a very long time.

For the first time since Ian had left Greenville, he had hope. Hope that he had found a friend in Jean. Hope for a new start and a new job, and amazingly, the saloon and the excitement of seeing new talent and watching their careers take off all seemed to appeal to him.

And for the first time in a couple of days, he smiled and truly meant it. "Okay! If you'll have me," Ian said, "I'll take you up on your offer. But please make me one promise."

Jean gave him a questioning glance.

"If I don't pull my weight around here, you won't hesitate to give me the boot. You are the only friend I have, and I expect honesty from you."

Jean agreed and came out from behind the bar, gave him a big hug, and held him until he broke the embrace. He was starting to fill up with tears again, and he didn't want to cry in front of his new friend.

Ian turned and headed for the door.

"See you tomorrow," Jean yelled. "Two o'clock sharp."

Ian turned his head ever so slightly, nodded, and smiled. "I'll be here."

On the drive back to the motel, his mind was racing. What had he just agreed to? Was Nashville—and a new job—what he needed? When he got back to the motel, he stripped down to his underwear and slid under the threadbare sheets. As he closed his eyes, his last thoughts were of Todd Slocum.

THE NEXT day Ian moved into his new home. His studio over the saloon was small but neat and clean. It contained a double bed, a chest of drawers, a couple of bedside tables, and a club chair. The kitchenette was tiny but adequate, and the attached bathroom had a stall shower, a toilet, and a pedestal sink. He couldn't believe how much he appreciated having a place to belong.

In an effort to familiarize Ian with the layout behind the bar and to get him proficient on their computer system, Jean had him begin bartending in the late afternoons, when the bar was just opening and pretty quiet. When it got busy, she had him at the front door as a bouncer.

It didn't take him long to fall into the rhythm of the bar business, and much to his surprise, he liked it.

But mostly he liked working with the new talent and getting them set up and ready for rehearsals and sound and lighting checks.

Jean told him on more than one occasion that he seemed to have a knack for knowing who would be a hit and who would be a flop. And with that, it wasn't long before she had him involved in the previewing, hiring, and scheduling of the singers and bands. Everything seemed to be working out and with each day, Ian felt a little of the weight he'd been carrying slowly start to melt away.

Every night Jean took special care to introduce Ian to all of her friends, regulars, and business contacts. And in no time at all, Ian was making quite a name for himself as Jean's right hand. One night, Jean called Ian over to introduce him to a good friend. "Ian. This is Josh Randal. Josh is a talent scout for Capitol Records, Nashville."

Josh shook Ian's hand. "Pleased to meet you. Jean's told me quite a lot about you."

Ian gave Jean a questioning glance and smiled. "Has she now?" he said looking back at Josh.

Jean blushed just a little. "Oh, don't be silly. Just in normal conversation," she responded. "So, Josh," Jean added, apparently wanting to change the topic. "What brings you in tonight?"

Josh explained he was doing his normal rounds, checking out clubs looking for new talent, and had saved his favorite career launcher for last. He gave Jean a kiss on the cheek.

Jean flashed that great big smile just as one of the barbacks tapped her on the shoulder. "Sorry to interrupt, Jean, but someone is asking for you at the front door."

"No problem, honey, I'll be right there," Jean replied. "Ian, while I'm gone, why don't you give Josh a lineup of the talent we have scheduled for the next couple of weeks."

"Absolutely," Ian said.

For over an hour, Ian went on about the solo artists and groups he and Jean had auditioned over the last couple of months and who they'd signed on to perform at the saloon. Of the groups he'd seen, he meticulously explained to Josh who he thought was going to make it and who wasn't and why.

After Ian had given Josh a complete rundown, he looked at his watch. "Man, where has the time gone? I need to get back to my post before Jean fires my chatty butt."

Josh chuckled. "Jean speaks very highly of you, so I'm pretty sure your job is safe."

"She is a doll and a half, and I owe her so much, I can't begin to tell you."

"That she is," Josh said. "It was really nice to meet you, and I'm sure I'll see you around."

"Same here, and I hope I didn't bore you too much with my ramblings."

"Not at all," Josh replied. "I love your enthusiasm."

The two men shook hands, and Ian headed back to the bar.

When he got back to his post, he watched Josh as he walked to the front door and said something to Jean. The two of them walked out together.

Forty-five minutes later, when Jean reappeared through the front door, Ian made a beeline for her. He took her gently by the arm and led her across the bar to a quiet corner.

Ian almost lifted her onto a barstool and looked her right in the eyes. "Okay, Anna Jean James. What was that all about?"

"All of what?" Jean replied.

Scotty Cade

"That didn't seem like a chance meeting to me," Ian quipped. "And besides… you were gone for a full forty-five minutes."

"Keeping track of me now, are you?" Jean asked.

"No. I'm just curious about what you're up to."

"Okay, fine," Jean admitted. "Josh had some questions about you. You know, how we met. If I thought you were honest and trustworthy. Just some things like that."

"Why in the world would Josh want to know these things about me?"

"If you must know," Jean said with a coy grin, "he's just been promoted, and he's looking for his replacement."

"What does that have to do—" Suddenly Ian's mouth dropped open and he wasn't sure he was hearing right. "—with me?" he finished.

Jean smiled broadly. "And he wanted to know if I thought you would make a good talent scout."

Ian felt a little weak in the knees. He looked around, found an empty bar stool, and took a seat. A million thoughts were running through his mind, and he was on major sensory overload. "I don't know anything about being a talent scout."

"I beg to differ," Jean said, patting his knee. "I've seen your keen eye when we've been auditioning new talent, and I personally believe you'd make a great scout."

"But I have no experience in the music industry."

"Josh knows that, and he thinks in this case, that might just be a plus."

"How so?"

"Look, honey. The music industry can be a tough, unforgiving business, and it can burn you out pretty quickly. With no experience, you wouldn't get caught up in all the drama and politics, and you'd bring a fresh approach to the position. Knowing good talent when you see it is not something you can be taught. You either have it or you don't, and personally… I think you have it."

Ian was really having a hard time believing what he was hearing. *Me. In the record business?*

Jean patted Ian again on the knee. "Now don't go getting too far ahead of yourself," she suggested. "It's not a done deal. The label still has to approve it, and he said it might be a tough sell."

Ian's excitement turned immediately to dejection. "What am I thinking," he said. "That makes perfect sense. Of course they would want someone with experience."

"But...," Jean added, "if I thought you were a good fit, he was willing to take on the fight."

Ian didn't know what to think, and he struggled to keep his emotions intact. His heart was so full. This woman, whom he'd met in a bar, who had given him a job and a place to live, not to mention a new start, was now recommending him for a talent scout position with a major record label?

Jean must have seen him struggling to keep himself composed. She smacked him on the leg. "Come on, we've gotta get back to work. We'll have plenty of time to talk about this later."

TWO DAYS later Ian got a call from Josh, and although he was still doubtful, he agreed to a meeting to discuss the opportunity. Josh was very persuasive, and by the end of the conversation, he had Ian believing he might actually be able to pull this off. But they still had the label to convince.

After many planning sessions and a lot of instruction, Josh finally set up a time to introduce Ian to the label executives. Ian wasn't sure if it went well or not, but he answered all the questions as honestly as he could, told them about the talent at the saloon just like he had done with Josh, and expressed how thankful he was for the opportunity.

THREE WEEKS passed and Ian hadn't heard a word from Josh or the label, so he was resigned to the fact that they just didn't want to risk the position on someone with no experience. And if the truth were told, he totally got that. Besides, he was happy at the saloon and was very grateful for the opportunity Jean had given him.

One afternoon just after opening, Josh showed up unannounced. Ian and Jean both saw him at the same time and glanced at one another nervously as they walked in his direction. When they came together, Josh stuck out his hand. "Welcome to Capitol Records Nashville."

"What? I got the job?"

"You got the job," Josh assured him. "If you still want it, that is."

"Oh, congratulations," Jean said wrapping her arms around Ian.

"Hell yeah, I still want it. I accept," Ian said, pumping Josh's hand.

Moments later Ian's expression changed. He looked around the saloon and realized he wouldn't be working for Jean any longer. He knew they would always be friends, but he also knew that things would be different. He and Jean had become very close, and in a way, she had become his surrogate mother. He wanted her, needed her, in his life.

Jean immediately picked up on the mood change. "What's wrong, honey?"

"I'm sure gonna miss this place." Ian paused and took a quick look around again and then focused on Jean. "And you."

Jean wrapped her arms around him again. "Then stay."

Ian placed his hands on Jean's shoulders and gently pushed her back so he could look her in the eyes. "You think I shouldn't take the job?"

"No!" Jean said. "Take the job but continue to work here. That way you can have the best of both worlds. I mean, if you want to, that is?"

Ian picked Jean up and spun her around. "Of course I want to."

"Then this is your home as long as you want it to be," Jean whispered.

Ian knew that eventually he would have to venture out on his own, but all in good time. *Baby steps, Ian. Baby steps.*

IAN THREW himself into his new job at Capitol with a vengeance and never looked back. Nine years went by since he'd left South Carolina, and not once did his parents try to contact him, although Todd tried a couple of times in the beginning. Ian was twenty-nine years old, and even now, so many years later, the pain of Todd's betrayal still cut deep at the slightest recollection. But he was living a full life, and he was happy… or so he thought.

His life was about to change in more ways than he could ever have believed possible.

Don't miss

When hunky aspiring country singer Billy Eagan heads to Nashville in search of his big break, a relationship and love are the furthest things from his mind. Taking a foreman's job at the Lazy H ranch and not knowing how he will be accepted, Billy decides to fly under the radar and stay as closeted as he can without denying who he really is. It's immediately confirmed that he made the right decision when he discovers that homophobia is still alive and well in Tennessee.

Then Billy gets his break and meets gorgeous record label executive Ian Dillon. Their worlds collide both professionally and personally, and Billy falls hard. But Ian is still haunted by the mysterious betrayal of his one and only lover, and knowing Billy possesses the power to emotionally destroy him, Ian decides to cut his losses and simply walk away. Determined not to give up on the man he loves, Billy secretly starts to unravel the past and quickly finds that it's not what it appears. Can Billy rescue Ian's heart, or will bigotry and hatred win over love?

http://www.dreamspinnerpress.com

SCOTTY CADE left Corporate America and twenty-five years of marketing and public relations in 2004 to buy an inn & restaurant on the island of Martha's Vineyard with his husband of nearly twenty years.

He started writing stories as soon as he could read, but only recently for publication. When not at the inn, you can find him on the bow of his boat writing romance novels with his Shetland sheepdog, Mavis, at his side. Being from the South and a lover of commitment and fidelity, most of his characters find their way to long, healthy relationships, however long it takes them to get there. He believes that, in the end, the boy should always get the boy.

Scotty and his partner are avid boaters and live aboard their boat, spending the summers on Martha's Vineyard and winters in various locations down south.

Contact Scotty:
Website: http://www.scottycade.com
Facebook: https://www.facebook.com/scotty.cade
Twitter: @ScottyCade
E-mail: scotty@scottycade.com

After one very long tour of duty in Afghanistan and an honorable discharge from the USMC, Elijah Preston comes home to nothing. He barely scrapes up enough money for a cheap motel in Quantico, Virginia, with no money-making opportunities in sight. A chance encounter in a local Walmart finally gives Eli hope for employment. Elijah is ready to sign on with Royce Mackey's proposition... until he hears what's required. Royce operates a gay military porn site and wants Eli as his next star, never mind that Eli isn't gay. Desperate and broke, Eli grudgingly accepts Royce's offer and soon finds himself immersed in a strange new world.

Hamish Turner's been there before. Taking Eli under his wing, he teaches him everything he can about Royce's operation. The two quickly become friends, easing the way for their first scene together. Awkward at first, they both ease into it and find there is more of a connection between them than either expected. Curious to see where their mutual attraction takes them, they begin a relationship off-screen. But life gets complicated when a crazed fan of Hamish's starts sending threatening letters demanding the scenes between the two men stop. Or else….

http://www.dreamspinnerpress.com

Leeland Jeffers is a contented single man with a thriving career in Atlanta. He's had a few unsuccessful relationships over the years, but no one has even come close to his first love, Harrison Rhinehart. They met in college when a mutual friend, Suzie Garrison, introduced Harry into their close-knit group. When the supposedly "straight" Harry made a move on Lee, the two men entered into a tumultuous secret love affair. In their senior year, the relationship finally ended when Harry informed Lee he was marrying Suzie.

Since graduation, the college friends have drifted apart. However, an unexpected invitation to a destination wedding seems set to reunite them all. Lee's speculation on whether Harry and Suzie will make an appearance threatens to derail his attendance. But Lee decides the hell with it and makes plans to go, Harry Rhinehart or no Harry Rhinehart.

After six months of research, adventure seekers Bowen McAlister, Cyrus Curran, Duff Gentry, and Lockhart Dawson make their way to Boulder, Colorado, to explore the abandoned gold mine Ruby Lode. But when they arrive, Duff, a born psychic, senses something isn't quite right—and the closer they get, the more his unease grows.

Something long buried in the deep shafts and drifts of Ruby Lode makes its presence known by exposing dark, guarded secrets. Preying on the adventurers' weaknesses and insecurities, Ruby Lode's own destructive secret threatens their sanity, friendship, and ultimately their lives. Bo, Cy, Duff, and Lockey must work together to unravel the century-old mystery before they become another footnote in the mine's history.

http://www.dreamspinnerpress.com

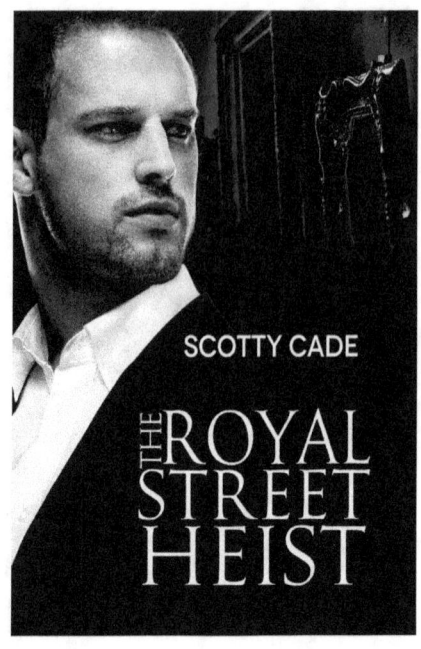

SCOTTY CADE

THE ROYAL STREET HEIST

When valuable Civil War era art is stolen from a popular New Orleans gallery, NOPD Lead Detective Montgomery "Beau" Bissonet and his partner set out to solve the crime. When the gallery's insurance company sends Tollison Cruz to the Big Easy to conduct their own independent investigation, personalities clash and battle lines are definitely drawn.

The heist quickly becomes a politically driven high profile case, and Detective Bissonet is furious when he's ordered to work along side Investigator Cruz to assure a timely arrest. The heat index soars to new levels when the two investigators discover they have a lot more in common than originally thought.

With the tension between them temporarily sated, Bissonet and Cruz finally start to work together, on more than just a professional level. But everything comes to a screeching halt when Beau discovers his cohort in crime has been withholding information regarding the investigation and has been concealing a very questionable past. What happens next rivals the scorching summer heat.

http://www.dreamspinnerpress.com

SCOTTY CADE

SUNRISE OVER SAVANNAH

Thompson and Caroline Gray were living their dream until Caroline's untimely death just two years after they'd bought the Thundercloud Marina. When Caroline died, she left Thompson alone and emotionally disconnected—until Thompson's longtime friend and towboat owner Hank Charming tows Garner Holt, a recently retired psychiatrist, and his boat into the marina for repair. Thompson and Hank are both drawn to the sailboat captain, but for very different reasons.

Since high school, Hank has secretly carried a torch for Thompson, even though Thompson remained committed to Caroline, even after her death. Hank is totally caught off guard when his initial attraction to Garner makes him realize this stranger might be the one to help him move on with his life. Thompson establishes a platonic friendship with Garner and starts to see the psychiatrist as his only lifeline to sanity. Life improves until Thompson sees Hank and Garner together, and old feelings Thompson thought were long buried begin to resurface. Garner quickly identifies the unresolved feelings between Hank and Thompson and decides to tap his professional skills and work behind the scenes to help Thompson and Hank see what has been right in front of them all along.

http://www.dreamspinnerpress.com

SCOTTY CADE

CHASING
THE
HORIZON

Needing a lifestyle change, Garner Holt, an uptight workaholic psychologist, buys a sailboat and trades in his prestigious job in New York City for a life on the water. After engine failure and six weeks in Savannah, Georgia for repair, he arrives in Key West, Florida early one morning and encounters a half-dressed hooligan walking along the docks of the marina. Garner immediately thinks this barefoot and shirtless man with a shaved head, multiple tattoos, and piercings in every orifice is going to rob him. He prepares for the worst. Instead, the stranger passes Garner by and climbs on a boat a few slips down. With the threat of danger gone, Garner is surprisingly intrigued.

Hawken Bristol is used to being on the receiving end of stereotypes. He sees the fear on the stranger's face, recognizes the rigidity in his stance, but is too tired from his wild night of partying to engage the frightened stranger. A few cat and mouse encounters around town lead to an uncanny attraction. However, after Garner helps Hawken dock his boat in a windstorm, sparks start to fly. But this new liaison brings up old baggage that threatens to derail everything they have going.

http://www.dreamspinnerpress.com

AN
UNCONVENTIONAL
COURTSHIP
Scotty Cade

Tristan Moreau loves his job as chief administrative officer and personal assistant to Webber Kincaid, President, Chairman, and CEO of Kincaid International. It would be the perfect job… if only he hadn't fallen in love with his boss as well as the work. After two years, he's still doing everything in his power to keep his feelings hidden—mostly because he wants to protect the reputation of his famous boss but also because he wants to keep his job.

Webber Kincaid has stayed in the closet, using his best friend and confidante as his beard. Everything in his life was working out just fine until he met Tristan Moreau. Within months, Tristan stole his heart and became his lifeline. But Webber knows the rules of the workplace better than anyone, so he's kept his distance.

But two years is too long to wonder "what if?"—especially when business takes them to a private Caribbean island. When Tristan and Webber succumb to the tropical heat, their professionalism starts to backslide. It's a seemingly impossible relationship, making a go at it under the paparazzi's microscope. It may be the best—or the worst—business decision they ever made.

http://www.dreamspinnerpress.com

AN
*Un*CONVENTIONAL
UNION
Scotty Cade

Kincaid International Corporation's CEO, Webber Kincaid, and his executive assistant, Tristan Moreau, have just returned from a Caribbean business trip gone horribly right. After years of hiding their love for each other, they finally came clean—and discovered KIC's chief financial officer has been up to some shady business transactions. Now that they're back, Tristan and Webber must expose the CFO's indiscretions—and save Webber's reputation, since he's ultimately responsible for his CFO's actions. With Tristan by his side, Webber faces KIC's board of directors and a looming investigation by the Securities and Exchange Commission and Department of Justice.

With all the uncertainty surrounding them, Webber and Tristan rely on the strength of their connection. Together, they plan an intimate wedding on the island of Martha's Vineyard. But despite their love for one another, Webber and Tristan quickly realize they have some hurdles to cross before they can start their unexpected new life.

http://www.dreamspinnerpress.com

Love Series

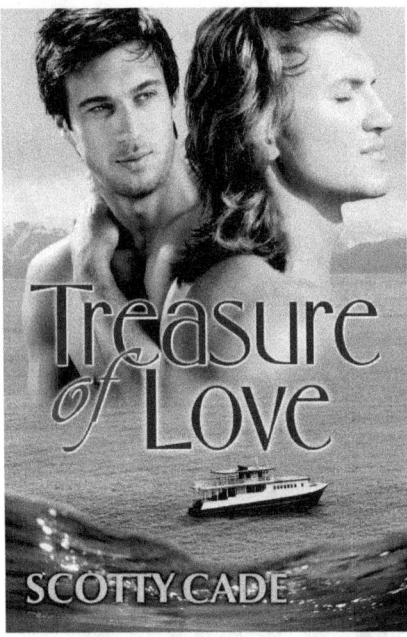

http://www.dreamspinnerpress.com

FOR **MORE** OF THE **BEST** GAY ROMANCE

DREAMSPINNER
PRESS
dreamspinnerpress.com

www.ingramcontent.com/pod-product-compliance
Lightning Source LLC
Chambersburg PA
CBHW060056260626
47160CB00005B/1693